ONLY THE STARS KNOW HER NAME

SALEM'S LOST STORY
OF
TITUBA'S DAUGHTER

AMANDA MARRONE

YELLOW
JACKET

YELLOW JACKET

an imprint of Little Bee Books

251 Park Avenue South, New York, NY 10010
Text copyright © 2019 by Amanda Marrone
All rights reserved, including the right of reproduction
in whole or in part in any form.
Yellow Jacket and associated colophon are trademarks
of Little Bee Books.
Manufactured in the United States of America MAP 0719
First Edition

1 3 5 7 9 10 8 6 4 2
Library of Congress Cataloging-in-Publication Data
is available upon request.
ISBN 978-1-4998-0890-2

yellowjacketreads.com

For Kerry Malloy,
big sister extraordinare
—AM

CHARACTERS

VIOLET: Born in Salem, Massachusetts, to Tituba and John, Arawak Indians enslaved by Samuel Parris. Although raised in the same house as the children in the Parris family, Violet was considered property and had to work hard. When the two girls she lived with accused her mother of witchcraft, she listened to her mother tell wild tales at the trial. After the witch trials, her parents were sold in 1693 and taken to parts unknown.

TITUBA: An Arawak Indian from South America, Tituba was captured and taken to Barbados, where she was sold into slavery. Samuel Parris brought her and her husband, John Indian, to Massachusetts, where they had a daughter, Violet. In 1692, Tituba was accused of witchcraft by two of her charges, Betty Parris and Betty's cousin, Abigail Williams. Instead of denying the charges, she wove a tale of sorcery and pointed fingers that set a wave of other accusations in motion. She later recanted her confession from prison, claiming it had been beaten out of her by Reverend Parris. When the governor of Massachusetts pardoned the accused, the reverend refused to pay her bail, and Tituba was sold from her jail cell, along with her husband, to an unnamed man. They never returned to Salem.

JOHN INDIAN: Husband to Tituba and father of Violet; enslaved by Samuel Parris. He was sold along with his wife after the Salem witch trials.

REVEREND SAMUEL PARRIS: Husband to Elizabeth Parris, father of Thomas and Betty, uncle of Abigail Williams. Born in London, Parris took over his father's sugar plantation in Barbados, where he purchased Tituba and her husband, an enslaved man, John Indian. In 1688, Parris was appointed the Puritan minister to Salem. Known for his cold demeanor, the reverend was not well liked there and had frequent contract disputes and arguments with the community.

ELIZABETH PARRIS: Wife to Samuel Parris, mother of Thomas and Betty, and guardian and aunt of Abigail Williams.

BETTY PARRIS: Daughter of Samuel and Elizabeth Parris. She was cared for by Tituba, alongside her cousin, Abigail Williams, and Tituba's daughter, Violet. After suffering fits and visions, Betty accused Tituba of bewitching her and Abigail.

ABIGAIL WILLIAMS: After her parents died, Abigail was sent to live with her relatives, the Parrises. She was raised by them and cared for by Tituba. Like Betty, she suffered from fits and claimed to be bewitched. Once, she thrust her hands into the coals of a fire. Abigail accused Tituba of witchcraft.

THOMAS PARRIS: Son of Samuel and Elizabeth Parris. Older brother to Betty.

ELIZABETH PRINCE: Orphaned after her mother, Sarah Osborne, was put in jail for witchcraft and died there. Elizabeth was left in the care of her stepfather, Alexander

Osborne. Elizabeth's mother was among the first three women accused of witchcraft in Salem. Sarah vehemently denied any wrongdoing.

TAMMY YOUNGER: A teen from Gloucester, who lost her parents when she was young, Tammy worked in various houses as a servant. Tammy was tutored to be a folk woman—to use magic as a healing art or a way to make money—by Martha Wilds; she made her way to Salem to form a coven to use the power and anger inside her, hoping to reach the top of Salem society.

SHERIFF GEORGE CORWIN: The sheriff signed all of the warrants for those accused and convicted of witchcraft during the trials. Corwin often claimed the property of the accused and split it with his deputies. He was particularly ruthless in the death of Giles Corey—a man in his late seventies—who was pressed to death under a great weight of rocks.

CHAPTER ONE

The Devil came to me and bid me to serve.
—TITUBA, FROM COURT TESTIMONY, 1692

Salem, Massachusetts
April 1693

s I neared Salem Village with Mistress Parris, I wondered if Mama might be back when I got home. Had she been freed from prison? Was she already settled into her familiar routine? Maybe her apple cakes would be sizzling in the pot?

It had been months since all the accused had been acquitted by none other than Governor Phips, so surely, she would be home by now.

She had to be.

As the cart bumped along the road, I hugged my arms

around myself and pretended they were Mama's arms.

It had been so long since I'd felt her arms around me. So long since she braided my hair or slipped a sugar candy in my hand when no one else was looking.

Most of all, I missed Mama's voice. I missed hearing about her people, the Arawak, and the mystical creatures that inhabited their land. Though she had been bought by Reverend Parris in Barbados, Barbados was not her home. She said she would wish on the North Star every night that she could turn into a dolphin so she could dive into the ocean and be back on her shore in a short day's swim.

But Mama was not a dolphin, and Barbados was where she worked hard until the reverend forced her to sail north to Massachusetts, where the work *and* the winters were hard.

But Mama still remembered her homeland and she'd seen more beautiful things than the people around here could ever imagine. Above all, Mama was a storyteller. She brought those strange lands to life, coloring the often-gray, unforgiving place we lived in bright, tropical sunsets. So vivid and delicious were her stories, I imagined them as dreams she'd plucked from my head and dipped in sweet molasses. And when winter months chilled us to our core, Mama warmed us with sky-blue waters and chattering monkeys eating fruit ripe for the picking all the year long.

Like the mischievous monkeys Mama spoke of, Betty, Abigail, and I always laughed at her stories, but mostly we marveled at the magic she said could foretell the future or reveal our one true love.

"Mama Tituba," Betty once asked, "will I marry Edward Hutchinson or Joseph English?"

Mama smiled, her full, brown cheekbones rising. "Those the boys who caught your fancy today, Betty?"

We laughed because, even at the tender age of nine, new boys were always catching Betty's fancy. Mama made sure Mistress Parris was nowhere in sight, and then carefully cracked an egg on the table. With skill, she plopped the white of the egg into a glass of water. We all peered into the glass to watch the white twisting in the liquid, waiting for Mama to make her proclamation.

"Looks like a horseshoe," Mama whispered finally. "Edward Hutchinson was selling a foal with his father just a few days ago; surely, he's your man." Mama brought the glass to her lips and swallowed its contents in one gulp. "But don't be telling your mother I wasted an egg on the likes of that boy, or there'll be hell to pay."

We gaped at Mama for using such language and then dissolved into new fits of laughter. Despite the different colors of our skin, despite having been born of three different mothers, we three girls lived under Reverend Parris's roof and—for a time—felt like sisters. We were bonded by Mama's tantalizing secrets so exciting from our everyday life, and we spread her stories to the girls in town and made divining potions of our own out of sight of watchful eyes.

We reveled in it all until we didn't.

One day, Betty and Abigail started telling stories of their own—dark ones—about Mama and other people. When that happened, folks were sent to Gallows Hill.

Many of them died.

Mama's stories were as light as the hint of salt in sea air, but after Betty's and Abigail's fits and finger-pointing, Mama started telling new tales that set the hair on the back of our necks on end. She talked of meeting with Satan himself and signing the Devil's book.

I'm still not sure I know the truth about how Betty and Abigail came to be afflicted. I still can't believe Mama had any part in it, but Mama confessed to having done just that.

It is something that weighs heavily on me. How could things ever get back to the way they were when Abigail and Betty remained carefree and Mama sat in jail close to thirteen months now?

I bit my lip. I had watched Mama tell those terrifying stories in front of the judge in the meetinghouse. My heart had raced hearing the words coming out of her mouth. Words of witchcraft and the Devil and flying through the night on poles.

I had watched girls pointing at things I couldn't see. I watched them claim that friends and neighbors were poking them with sewing needles and sending out their spectral selves to wrap their hands around their necks.

And then I watched as Mama was loaded into a cart with Sarah Good and Sarah Osborne to be taken to jail in Boston—all three of whom Betty and Abigail had accused of bewitching them.

"Serves the reverend right, bringing Indians into our

town," Mistress Putnam had said to Mistress Lewis as if I weren't standing but three or four steps from them.

Mistress Lewis smiled slyly. "That Tituba sure taught him a lesson, though. He could have hired any number of local girls to work for him; he got what he deserved!"

Mistress Putnam narrowed her eyes at the crowd around us. "I suspect there shall be more in town who get what they deserve before the week's end."

My stomach felt punched by those words. No one in Salem knew Mama and Papa were Arawak except the Parris family—Mama and Papa were forbidden to talk about it and only did so when the reverend and mistress were not at home or out of earshot, but we were just Indians to everyone because we had brown skin. We were just *Indian* because that was the name Reverend Parris gave us. But I knew being Arawak or *Indian* didn't have anything to do with witchcraft. Besides, of the three women being carted away, Mama was the only Indian.

One could almost believe Sarah Good was a witch, though. She was begging around Salem with her five-year-old daughter in tow, muttering curses under her breath at even those who had a loaf of bread to share with her. That her young daughter was later accused, well, that was harder to reconcile.

But Sarah Osborne was more troubling—she had been ill in bed for over a year—too ill to even come to church services. Could a woman so sick as to miss services be out flying through the night on a pole or dancing in the woods with the Devil?

Could a woman who was so ill that she lasted but nine weeks in jail before her heart gave out really have been a vessel for the Devil's work?

And what of Mama? Yes, she had cracked eggs in water and made predictions. She had told me of her people, the Arawak, and their connection to the visible and non-visible worlds. She told me of the souls resting in the trees and rivers, and that rainbows formed a bridge between the earth and sky. She talked of the spirits of the forests, the Opias, who only came out at night. She talked of all these fantastical things, but not once had she ever mentioned the Devil.

But if what she said was true, how could she have done all those things without me noticing? Every night I heard her breathing in bed next to Papa, and every morning her boots were polished with not a hint of mud or forest leaf stuck to them.

The day the sheriff took Mama and Sarah Good and Sarah Osborne away in the cart, I watched Sarah Good's daughter try to pull from her father's hand to chase after it.

Sarah Osborne's daughter, Elizabeth Prince, fell to the dirt road and cried out to her mother, begging her to confess. My mother's brown eyes landed on mine and she held her head steady and high. She ran a finger down her curved nose that looked just like mine and then touched her full lips. She pointed to me as if I could somehow feel that kiss, but I wasn't sure I even wanted to, not after everyone in town had heard what she had done from those very same lips.

I wanted to hang my head in shame for thinking such thoughts, but I stiffened my spine and kept my head high, sure that this was all some sort of bad dream—a dream I was still waiting to wake up from. Because how could Mama really and truly be a witch?

I guess that this is my story, a story I am trying to figure out the ending to.

CHAPTER TWO

I do not know that the Devil goes about
in my likeness to do any hurt.
—SARAH OSBORNE

houghts of stories and Mama consumed me as Mistress Parris and I continued our ride back to Salem Village. We'd been near eight weeks caring for her brother's family in North Gloucester after the birth of a new boy. With five other children full of phlegm and bile, my days were full, but the long hours kept my mind from dwelling too deeply on my troubles.

I grabbed hold of the cart's side planks as it bumped along a part of the road mired in washboard ruts. Mistress Parris sat at the lead with her son, Thomas, and grabbed his arm to steady herself.

Thomas was a year older than me, and at age fourteen, he no longer paid me any mind except to make sure I darned his socks and that his monthly bathwater was warm.

The nearer we got to the parsonage, the heavier my heart weighed. I took in the greenery growing quick and lush along the path and gave praise to spring and its renewal to us all, but thoughts of being home without Mama made it hard to be truly thankful.

Many nights in Gloucester I dreamed that Reverend Parris had changed his mind and paid Mama's jail fee and she'd be waiting for me when we arrived back home. I dreamed I'd walk through the doors and she'd take me in her arms. It was a small hope that kept me going these last few weeks, though I knew deep down that even if he wanted to help, the reverend's salary would never have any extra coins. And even if he had, it was unlikely he would use them on Mama.

Chickadees flittered in the brush along the road and they reminded me of Mama; never pausing—happily chattering all day. I knew I would have to be satisfied with Papa's quiet company. In some ways he was like the reverend; they both seemed to have no great affection for children. Papa was more like a blue heron, though, moving slowing and thoughtfully along the water's edge, focused on completing his list of daily chores. Reverend Parris, with his pointed nose and steely eyes, reminded me of the red-tailed hawk: strident and hard and ready to tear flesh from the bone with its sharp beak.

At least I knew I could always count on a weary smile from Papa after bedtime prayers, and when the candle was blown out he'd remind me that even though Mama wasn't here, the North Star was shining down on her same as us.

Papa seemed to do his best talking after the candle was out. I suppose it was because he was finally free to let his mind ponder on his family without the reverend's list of chores cluttering his head.

Some nights, as sleep would just be taking hold, I'd hear Papa whisper about finding some extra work to earn money. Maybe more hours in Mr. Ingersoll's tavern, or being skilled with a hammer and nail, he might be sought out to repair our neighbors' fences and barns. He had plans to get Mama back, and as I'd drift off he'd whisper, "Patience is a virtue, Violet."

I had been more than patient and I hoped that while I

was away he'd been able to find that extra work. It seemed all I had these days was hope, and I prayed on that bumpy road that he'd earned the money to buy Mama her freedom.

When we finally pulled up to the parsonage, it was early evening, and though I was sure Papa would be back from gathering wood, I was careful not to show my excitement and neglect my work. The reverend, stony-faced as always, came out to greet us. I slung my satchel over my shoulder and took hold of a basket of parsnips and potatoes we'd been sent home with, nodded a greeting, and then brought them into the house.

I was thankful Betty and Abigail were nowhere in sight, but disappointed Papa was absent as well.

As soon as I'd stored away the root vegetables, I asked Mistress Parris if I could be excused to my room to recover from our long trip. She exchanged a look with the reverend that sent a nervous tickle bubbling up in the pit of my stomach.

"Sit down, Violet," the reverend said, pointing to the bench by the fire. "And, Thomas, please bring in some kindling."

Thomas left, but not before giving me a sideways look.

Gathering kindling was one of Papa's jobs since the town's people stopped catering to the reverend. As Thomas left, the nervous bubble in my stomach traveled up my spine.

The reverend motioned to the bench again, but my feet seemed to be stuck to the floor with pitch. The parsonage was too quiet, and all I could think was that something had happened to Mama—that she took ill in that jailhouse in Boston, or even died.

"I'll be arranging my things," Mistress Parris said softly, and as she made her way up the stairs, I caught a glimpse of Betty and Abigail peeking down from the darkness at the top; those girls were not known for their quiet, and the nervous tickle I felt spread like a wave through my whole body, causing the blood to thump loudly in my ears.

Not sure I would be able to stand much longer, I made my way to the bench and gripped the edges as tightly as I could.

The reverend was never one to mince his words and I knew the news would be delivered swiftly. "Violet, you know our town has weathered a stormy period and we are still finding our footing. You will be greatly relieved to hear that as part of that process your parents have been purchased and your mother is no longer in confinement."

My heart just about beat out of my chest and I grinned ear to ear. It was no surprise to me that someone in town had seen what a hard worker Mama was and had paid her bail. I knew Papa was surely with her and I was ready to gather my things and join them; soon we'd all be sleeping under that North Star together as a family again.

"As you are a valuable worker in our home," he continued, "we have chosen to keep you here with us. I am sure the news of your mother's release is a blessing to you from God and your parents will be an asset to their new household."

My hopes felt like they were torn from the bone and swallowed whole. "Who bought them?" I asked, trembling. "Where did they take them?"

The reverend shrugged carelessly. "A man traveling north. Your parents are good laborers and will no doubt earn their keep. As I said, it is a blessing and we should thank the Lord tonight in our prayers."

My body turned to ice and spasms racked my body.

A *blessing?*

Mama and Papa were *gone.*

Sold.

And I was left behind.

I stumbled to the room we had shared and clung to the threshold. While I'd been in Gloucester caring for this family's kin, *my* family had been wrenched from me and the room we shared cleared of their few belongings.

I flung myself on their bed. The pillows still carried the faint smell of Papa's pipe and the lavender Mama used to keep the linens fresh during the long winter months. A painful wail poured from deep inside me as I pounded the bed.

"When you have composed yourself, you will need to get dinner started and the table set," Reverend Parris called out from the main room.

And that was it.

No goodbyes.

No apologies.

No anything.

It was like Mama and Papa never were. It was like I should just move on and not feel their absence.

"Did you hear me, Violet? Mistress Parris needs you to get dinner started while she rests from the long trip."

As I stared wildly about the small room in the gathering darkness, a black shadow filled me, as if I were pulling the night inside to fill the space where my scream had come. Tonight, there would be no quiet whispers from my father—no talk of the North Star.

I heard footsteps loudly coming my way. And then I felt Reverend Parris's presence in the doorway. "Violet!"

I slowly turned his way. "I heard you," I said, through gritted teeth, eyes narrowed on his hawkish face. "And I will be out in a minute."

I rolled over and sat on the bed with my back to him, knees drawn tight to my chest. His steps, quieter now, retreated from the doorway. My tears dried, and anger welled up in all the places that used to hold hope.

I had wondered how my mother could make such terrible accusations against the people of Salem Village. I had wondered if they were true and, if not, how she could live with herself knowing how many people had died.

Now I finally understood.

We were never truly a part of this family. I had no sisters under this roof. Mama and Papa and I, we were simply hearth sweepers, chicken pluckers, cleaners of chamber pots—property.

But now I was also ready to take on the mantle of *witch*; and if the Devil had come to me then and there and asked me to sign his book, I would have done so in my very own blood.

Or that of Reverend Parris's.

CHAPTER THREE

I took more than a minute, perhaps even ten, before I willed myself to rise from my parents' bed. The Parris family could well wait for their supper or make it themselves.

My eyes were puffy—I had to view everything through mere slits—and no doubt the whites were red. I had seen Abigail's eyes when she first arrived at the Parris house after her parents' deaths. It was like the blood from her heart had leaked into her eyes. I imagined mine looked like that as well now.

Mama had welcomed Abigail when she walked through our door, though, wrapping her tiny frame tight in her long arms as she cried for her parents. Mama, in hushed tones, whispered and promised her it would be all right. She told Abigail she would be there for her any time of any day and all she had to do was call out for Mama Tituba.

And Mama *was* there for her, and for me and Betty as well.

And now it was *my* turn—now *I* was the orphan—only there was no one to wrap their long arms around me. Mistress Parris certainly never took on the role of mother after Mama was sent to jail.

Though I didn't want to give the Parris family the satisfaction of seeing how wounded I was, I knew there was nothing to be done about it.

I had no magic to cast a spell that would take away the pain that was surely showing on my face, nor soothe my swollen eyes.

My heart raced, and anger and loss washed over me again until even the tips of my ears burned with heat.

Let them see me! Let them see the heartache I wear on my face, and every tear that falls down my cheeks.

I will look at each of them in their cold eyes and they

will see what they have done.

New sobs racked my body. These people will surely come to see how wrong it is, and perhaps it will soften their hearts.

How could it not?

So many children in Salem and those up and down the coast were orphans from disease and attacks. So many parents wasted away in their beds for no reason the doctors could find. The land was unforgiving, but I was willing to forgive this family if they could find it in their hearts to see how wrong they were, to see the terrible injustice that had been done to me.

Who could be so unfeeling as to separate a child from their parents on purpose? Once they saw my face, they would know they had to fix this.

And perhaps I was misjudging Mistress Parris—she could have been as surprised as I. Perhaps she walked through the door thinking Papa was still here. Perhaps she will think about how her children would feel if they lost her.

Perhaps Abigail, who lost her own parents, will tell the reverend how wrong it was to sell my parents without me, and that I should be reunited with them at once.

Abigail owed that much to me after what she had done.

My face crumpled.

I knew I was dreaming to think that Abigail could actually find the nerve to speak on my behalf against the reverend.

She hadn't spoken but commands to me since the accusations began.

Since Mama went to jail.

And Betty, she was far worse. As the days and months had passed, she grew more and more callous, more demanding. But perhaps Betty would remember that we had once been sisters and feel for me and insist her parents send me north.

I stoked the fire and put a salted pork loin in the pot. It would not be ready for our normal suppertime, and I frowned, thinking Betty and Abigail had surely been capable of having started it themselves, but they remained out of sight.

Everyone was out of sight. Usually the main room was where everyone gathered and sewed and cooked and, in the case of the reverend, wrote his sermons.

Tonight, I was alone.

I chopped some root vegetables and seasoned the pot and then turned to the table.

Mama always made sure the napkins were folded precisely, no spills of cider on the tablecloth. She did so much, and I had wanted to do none of it, but tonight I knew I must. I had to be good and hope they saw just how good I was, and I hoped they changed their minds.

What else could I do to change their minds?

I looked around the room and started putting things back in place—yarn and needles in the basket, a shawl on its hook, boots lined straight against the wall.

I grabbed the broom and swept the ashes that had drifted out onto the floor.

What else?

I jumped when I heard steps on the stairs. Reverend Parris was making his way down followed by Betty and Abigail.

"Is dinner ready, Violet?" Betty asked casually, plopping down at her seat as if this were an ordinary evening. "'Tis quite late this evening, and I am famished."

"It can be forgiven tonight," the reverend said, "after all . . ."

My breath caught.

"You have had a long journey from Gloucester, but I will not be so generous tomorrow. Do you understand me?"

I stared at him, speechless, silently begging him to see what was right in front of him—could he not see how I ached? How could he ignore what he had done to me?

I turned to Betty, who sniffed and unfolded her napkin, her eyes turning impatiently toward the pot on the hearth.

"Abigail," I said softly, hoping at least she might show me some compassion, but she sat next to Betty and rearranged the silverware without a glance to me.

Before I knew what was happening, the reverend charged at me and I shrank as he grabbed my wrist. "Have you lost your hearing? I asked you, *do you understand, Violet?*" he demanded as his fingers squeezed painfully.

"Yes," I whispered, through clenched teeth.

"Excuse me?" he said, twisting my arm. "Perhaps now it is I who is hard of hearing."

"Yes!" I spat. "I understand, all too well."

He released me, and it was clear that he cared not that he'd sold my parents without even giving me a chance to say goodbye and it was clear I was not going anywhere, not if he had anything to do with it. I could never do enough odd jobs or scramble to earn enough coins to buy my freedom, and I would be stuck with this family forever—unless a miracle happened.

No.

Despite what the reverend preached, I no longer believed in miracles. If I were to find my parents, I could not depend on God to intervene—I would have to make my own miracle happen.

As I dished out the meat, I vowed then and there that I would rush through all my chores every day so I could go out into the woods and seek the tall man in the hat from Boston that Mama had spoken of while she was under interrogation. If he had come to her—sought her out in the middle of the night to make mischief for the Devil—surely, he would come to her daughter.

I had trembled along with the whole town when Mama

spoke of that strange man who appeared to her in our room one night. She said it was that man who told her to hurt the children of Salem—who told her to hurt Betty and Abigail. He asked her to sign the book.

I had been chilled to my bones to think such a specter had not only been in our house but in the very room in which I slept. And when Mama said the man turned into a large, black dog and then a bristled, talking pig, and finally into an imp just three feet high with a too long nose and covered from head to toe in coarse, black hair—I shook like a winter wind had swept through the meetinghouse and taken home in my soul.

That man and that creature—be they one and same or two different things—they haunted my dreams for months, but today, thinking of them, I could only smile.

Today I would gladly seek their company, and I would shake the hand of the tall man and thank him for seeking me out.

When he comes to me—and I was sure he would—when he holds out that dark book full of names, he won't even have to ask if I am ready to sign. I would grab the pencil out of his hands and make Betty Parris sorry she taught me how to read and write.

I would print my name in that book and strike out at the people in this house, because they are by far more terrifying than anything I might meet in the woods.

The tall man and the imp—I would welcome them any day instead of Reverend Parris.

CHAPTER FOUR

he next morning, I rose early with little appetite. I nibbled on bread that even honey could not sweeten. I was sure I had slept no more than an hour, as my mind had raced through the night, trying to figure out a way to find Mama and Papa, trying to find a way to make my miracle happen. As the moon traveled across the sky toward morning, I wondered if the tall man from Boston would indeed come to me.

A part of me thought he could just be a story Mama had told, because in the past year there had been no mention of witches or spells or strange men appearing at the foot of beds.

The man, as Mama had described, seemed so real at the time, so frightening. If he was real, though, why had no one talked of him these many months?

Maybe this tall man had simply tired of bedeviling the people of Salem and found another town in which to work the Devil's mischief.

I poked at the coals in the hearth and tried to wrap my mind around a reason Mama would have lied. But the day Betty and Abigail were afflicted, that is a day I will never forget.

It was no lie that Abigail Williams had raced around this very room, screaming and barking and pointing wildly in the air, before she reached into this very hearth, grabbed red-hot coals with her bare hands, and tossed them at Reverend Parris.

I'd had to mend the small holes burned into the reverend's clothes.

There were still scorch marks on the floor and scars on Abigail's palms.

Surely, liars would not go as far as to reach into a fire. And surely, liars would not have kept up the pretense of fits and barking for week after week if they were not truly afflicted.

But maybe they would.

I thought of our house. We walked on eggshells trying to guess what to do to please the reverend and Mistress Parris. We all feared the switch, though, me more than any of the others.

But maybe liars would think it best to continue the pretense rather than confess and be beaten—or thrown in the stocks—or both, even if it meant people went to jail.

Even if it meant people died.

Could someone lie and not care if people died as a result of that lie?

I had asked Betty and Abigail this very question on the day I heard that Mama had taken her confession back. Governor Phips had ordered an end to the arrests. I thought that if Betty and Abigail might confess to lying, the reverend would pay to bring Mama home.

***

I still remembered what happened, as clear as day. It was a quiet evening: Papa was at Ingersoll's Tavern working behind the counter, and Mistress Parris and the reverend were in town to argue that his contract wasn't being satisfied and that we had barely enough wood to stay warm the past winter.

Abigail and Betty were at home and both sewing, and though they were still treating me coolly, I was sure they would confess to me. I was sure they wanted Mama home as much as I did.

"Betty—Abigail, might I have a moment of your time?" I felt foolish at the formalness of my approach, but things were different now. I had to tread cautiously, especially around Betty.

Betty raised her nose in the air and sniffed, a habit of her mother's she had grown to use more and more. "You may have but a moment, Violet. We have to finish our stitches before Mother and Father come home."

Abigail lowered her hoop and looked to Betty, who rolled her eyes at her cousin.

"You have likely heard my mother has recently recanted her confession. She said it was all lies beaten out of her from your father and—"

"Lies, indeed!" Betty snapped. "Your mother is telling lies now, maligning my family's name all to get out of prison, despite what she did to us."

Heat rose to my face. "Perhaps your father did not beat the confession out of her, but . . ."

Betty stood, her stitching hoop clutched with white knuckles. "Your mother and Sarah Good and Sarah Osborne met with the tall man. They flew on poles to Boston, they sent their selves after Abigail and me, and we almost died!"

"Sarah Good and Sarah Osborne *did* die," I reminded her. "They did not confess. They told the court you were liars and they hung on Gallows Hill. So many hung on that hill."

Betty's cheeks flushed in anger while Abigail buried her face in her hands.

I ran to Betty and took the hoop gently from her hands and put it on the table. "Please, Betty. I will not judge you. I just want Mama home; I want things to be like they used to be. Remember how it used to be? We had fun and we laughed. I miss that. I miss you and Abigail. There has been no laughter since Mama was taken away. Your father might whip you with the switch, but would it not be worth it to have *Mama Tituba* home?"

"Betty," Abigail cried.

Betty sneered. "Your mother confessed because she was guilty. Why would she otherwise? *And think of all the other people who confessed!*" Betty yelled. "So many people confessed because it was all true! It was true and your mother is guilty and I'm glad she's gone so she cannot torment me again!"

She turned and stomped up the stairs to her room.

My breath hitched in my throat. "Abigail. Please say it wasn't true. I miss my mama. I miss her so, so much. Sometimes I'm afraid, since I've grown, she won't recognize me when I see her again."

Abigail shook her head and then looked down at her scarred palms. "The Devil made me reach into the fire that night."

"The Devil, but not Mama!" I insisted. "Please tell me it was not Mama!"

"Abigail!" Betty cried from the top of the stairs. "It is time for bed!"

Abigail stared past me. "The Devil, Mama Tituba, Sarah Good, and Sarah Osborne—they all came to me. They came to me and I put my hands in the fire to make them stop." She slowly turned and made her way up the stairs one halting foot step at a time.

"Abigail!" I cried. "Tell me the truth!"

She looked over her shoulder at me. "Your mother is a witch and I have the scars to prove it."

***

I heard some rustling from upstairs and blinked. The family was starting to rise to prepare for services. How long was I staring into the fire, how long ago was that evening I had just been thinking on?

I took a deep breath and started the morning preparations.

I threw some kindling on top of the coals and watched small flames start to grow. Whether Betty and Abigail were liars or victims, I needed to arm myself in case the tall man did not come for me, because I needed to find Mama and Papa however I could.

The reverend had said that my parents were taken up north, but I could wander for months or years and be no closer to finding them. I prayed that there was someone in town who had seen the man who bought Papa. Maybe someone had talked to the man or sold him something.

Surely, one of the busybody gossips in town had asked where John Indian was being taken.

At least I hoped someone had.

Today was the Sabbath, and though hardly anyone had spoken to me in months—since the first days my mother started pointing fingers—I was determined to embolden myself to ask someone, maybe everyone, if they knew where my parents had been taken.

CHAPTER FIVE

The rest of April and May, I walked through the woods gathering kindling for the Parris house as none in the town would provide it as the reverend's contract stipulated. It would have been Papa's job, but now it was mine.

I paused now and again to silence the cracking of twigs and leaves underfoot to listen, but the woods remained quiet except for the chatter of birds and the rustle of squirrels scavenging for food in the leaf litter.

I felt like half a person, unable to remember what it was to smile, to breathe without care.

No one in Salem seemed to know where my parents were

taken. I had even been so bold as to ask Sheriff Corwin, but that tall, dark man—one who made me think of the man in Mama's stories—just laughed at me.

Reverend Parris whipped me with a switch after he had heard I talked to the sheriff. And he whipped me again after he had heard I talked to so many others.

Soon, I decided to stop talking to people and start going down that other path. I had thought just wanting to sign the Devil's book would make him appear, but as the weeks passed, I questioned if what I thought was true. Doubt swirled in my head.

One day in early June, I put my bundle of sticks at the edge of the stream and stretched out on a flat rock that seemed made for resting. If the dark forces were real, why was I still alone in the woods?

I lay back and stared up into what little sky I could see through the treetops and I wondered how Mama and Papa were faring, wherever they were. I wondered if they could feel the ache I had from missing them.

I still couldn't make sense of it all.

Mama had said in front of the whole town that the

Devil had shown her how to fly on a pole in the night air. If I could fly on a pole, I would hover over the parsonage and dump a basket of rocks down the chimney and splash the stew onto the coals and then let the Devil take me to Mama and Papa and we could be a family again.

But if Mama could really fly, why hadn't she come to fetch me?

I closed my eyes and dug my fingernails into my palms. As each day passed, it was getting harder and harder to figure if Betty, Abigail, and even Mama were great liars or truly afflicted. Many people had whispered to both sides, but why would Mama have confessed to so many bad things if they weren't true?

"Violet Indian?"

I jumped clean out of my skin and cursed as my nervous feet kicked my kindling into the stream. I twisted around quick, half expecting to see Satan himself, but there was Elizabeth Prince and a girl I didn't know. My heart thumped hard in my chest as I marveled how they were able to sneak up on me so quietly. As one of the few people with color to her skin in Salem, I was used to eyes finding their way to me, but this strange girl stared so boldly and so intensely, I half wondered if she was the actual Devil in disguise sizing me up.

It had been months since I had last seen Elizabeth, but it was clear the passing of her mother had not sat well with her. She was thirteen, same as me, but her faded dress hung loosely around her now-skeletal frame. Her blond hair was tied up and hidden under a once-white cap that had yellowed with age and lack of washing. Her green eyes were rimmed in red and so sunken they almost looked as if she'd rubbed ash around them.

The other girl's brown, uncombed hair hung past her shoulders in greasy tangles like a beggar too poor for a brush or a cap. Her tan dress was worn and covered with tears she hadn't bothered to mend. She reminded me of an urchin who might beg for scraps in the streets, but her blue eyes looked down at me with the same airs of Mistress Parris and I wondered where she got such nerve.

"*Violet*," Elizabeth whispered, as if she were afraid someone might hear her way out in the woods, "this is *Tammy, Tammy Younger* from Common Settlement near Gloucester.

She saw you there with Mistress Parris."

Elizabeth nibbled nervously on her bottom lip as Tammy held out a hand to me. I cringed at the dirt caked under Tammy's nails. She waved her fingers at me impatiently, and though this wild girl made me feel unbalanced, I let her help me up. I casually brushed the moss and leaves off the back of my dress and hoped she couldn't hear the blood pumping loudly in my ears.

She folded her arms across her chest and looked me up and down. "Violet Indian, I heard your mother is a confessed witch. Are you a witch as well?"

My jaw dropped, and I shook my head. "No! Of course not! And my mother recanted her confession."

Despite just a few minutes ago wishing to sign the Devil's book, Tammy's asking that question brought back a flood of nightmares.

Afflicted girls bewitched and screaming; their fingers pointing. Names were cast about and then people were cast in jail.

Mama told tales.

Necks snapped on Gallows Hill.

A man was pressed to death under the weight of rocks put on him by Sheriff Corwin.

It had been a long time since Governor Phips pardoned the last of the accused and it seemed people were content to pretend none of it ever happened. Betty and Abigail certainly went on with their Bible study and needlework and flirtations with boys.

But being asked if I were a witch, well, it made the air close in around me and I could almost feel the noose tightening around my neck. It was one thing to seek the Devil in private and quite another to call myself a *witch* out loud.

Tammy Younger glared daggers at Elizabeth, who seemed to want to hide in that oversized dress she wore. Elizabeth gave a faint shrug and looked down at her scuffed boots. "I never said she was a witch. I just said maybe."

I watched this exchange and slowly realized they weren't accusing me of witchcraft in a way that would be followed by fits and writhing and swinging at Gallows Hill—these girls were hoping I really was a witch.

But why?

My first instinct was to run straight back to the parsonage

and forget the greasy-haired girl with the piercing blue eyes, but I had so many questions about witches and Mama that it almost seemed like fate brought her to me.

Tammy frowned, kicked a small rock toward me, and then turned, walking briskly toward town. Elizabeth gave me a quick, nervous glance and then took off after her.

As they moved noisily through the woods away from me, a panic inside me grew. Suddenly, I was overwhelmed with the thought that this Tammy could help me, and I *had* to make sure she did.

"Wait!" I called out.

Elizabeth reached out to Tammy and they stopped. Tammy slowly turned to me with her hands on her hips. "Yes, Violet Indian?"

"Why did you want to know if I was a witch? And . . ." I swallowed hard. "And even if I were, why would I tell someone the likes of you?" I added the last bit to make sure she knew I wasn't so impressed with her and her haughty ways.

It was clear Tammy Younger was not accustomed to being talked to in such a manner. She was unrefined for sure, but I could tell she didn't let that stop her from getting what she wanted or being treated with respect.

She cocked her head and walked slowly toward me. She smiled warmly, but I dared not let my guard down. If she thought I had overstepped my boundaries, I was sure this strangely powerful girl might give me a whipping worse than being switched by Reverend Parris.

Tammy stopped a mere foot from me, and though I felt the need to step back, I held my ground.

"You can relax, Violet Indian. I just wanted to know if you were a witch and if you might want to join our coven."

CHAPTER SIX

I never saw the Devil's book nor knew that he had one.
—ANN PUDEATOR

To hear the word *coven* said aloud chilled me despite the heat. I was shocked at how brazen this girl could be, but Tammy saw my face and laughed. "No need to fret, Violet Indian." She shot a look at Elizabeth, whose hands were trembling. "Like I have told *her* repeatedly, people don't bother about witches no more."

She waved her fingers dismissively in the air. "We have a few women up in Gloucester—they live on the outskirts and curse the townsfolk and travelers if they won't throw them a coin or a bite to eat. No one even thinks of locking them up, and they even earn bread and eggs by making love potions and future casting."

I thought of Mama and her future casting. Cracked eggs or the color of the sky could tell us our future husband or how many children we might have. Before I could even conjure up Mama's face in my mind, Tammy moved on me like a dog on a rat, snatching my wrist and holding it firm. "Do you feel that, Violet Indian? Do you feel that power in me?"

My eyes widened. I had taken Tammy Younger's hand a short time ago, but now it seemed to contain lightning. I felt a jolt travel from her hand to me that made the hair on my arm stand at attention.

She let go and nodded; her eyes stayed locked on mine. "Martha Wilds knew I was filled with a powerful anger and she showed me how to gather it up and make an *actual* storm inside me."

"Like when you're hollow and nothing but shadows fill your insides?" I whispered.

Her blue eyes glowed. "Yes! Martha said that anger opens the door to magic and we just have to walk through and then we can work mischief on those pious hypocrites who steal land from their neighbors and beat their servants."

"Have you met . . . the Devil?" I asked, knowing it was something I wanted and feared all at the same time.

"No." Tammy flipped her greasy hair over her shoulders. "Martha Wilds says we don't need to meet the Devil. She said what we have is more folk-women magic, anyway. You know, magic from the earth and water and air."

Elizabeth nodded. "That Martha Wilds woman told Tammy that the Devil can't be bothered to show his face to the likes of us mortals. He's too busy making his own mischief!"

I frowned. "Can't be bothered? My mama said she met the Devil, and she wasn't the only one."

I looked to Elizabeth, but she bowed her head. Her mother had made no such confession before she had died in prison.

Tammy rolled her eyes and accompanied the gesture with a choking laugh. She walked around me, lightly tracing a finger across my shoulders, causing the hairs on my arm to stand on end. "Oh, so naïve. People tell tales, Violet Indian, but I'd wager those tales were told to keep necks out of the hangman's noose. I'd also wager you have some anger inside you. I'd wager your backside is covered in switch marks, unless that reverend of yours prefers to teach his lessons with an open palm."

She narrowed her eyes. "No. I can see it all on your face; *he* is partial to the switch."

I hated that she could somehow reach inside my head and steal my thoughts. Reverend Parris was quick to use a switch. Betty and Abigail had felt its sting, but I had known its bite.

Tammy dashed away from me and broke a branch off a sapling. She swished it sharply, and I flinched as it cut through the air. "Mrs. Sewall preferred a willow switch—we had a tree a few steps from the riverbank out back of the yard—but Mr. Sewall's open palm could make stars dance in your eyes. They took me in after my folks died of pox. I thought it was out of kindness, but I soon found out they knew *nothing* of kindness."

Elizabeth nodded. "She ran away from them—all the way to Salem. I found her sleeping in our barn with the new batch of kittens."

Tammy snapped the switch she was holding in two and threw the pieces aside. "When you came to Gloucester, there was talk aplenty. Few Indians like you working for the folk up there or anywhere, but people said your mother spread the craft around Salem and that started the madness. Folks said she brought it here from some island that the reverend bought her from."

I felt a heat rise in my brown cheeks. People towns over were talking about Mama? "It was Betty and Abigail who started the madness," I said defiantly. "My mother . . ."

I paused. What *had* Mama done?

Tammy laughed again. "It's fine, Violet Indian, your mother just—"

I was suddenly enraged and before I knew what I was doing, I pushed Tammy to the ground. "Stop calling me *Indian! That is not my name!* I don't . . . I don't *have* a last name. That's just what they called us because they couldn't be bothered to give us a proper one. I am an Arawak but that's not my name either, it is just what I am. What my parents are."

Tammy's eyes flashed with anger and I tensed myself for

a fight, but then she shook her head and licked her parched lips. "I knew you were worth the walk to Salem, Violet *Somebody*." She pushed herself up to sitting and patted the leaf litter, motioning for Elizabeth and me to join her.

I thought she'd be outraged by what I'd done, but instead she waited calmly as if she was on the ground under her own volition. Elizabeth plopped herself down like an obedient dog, but I took my time folding my skirts and sitting just a bit off from the two.

"Thing is, people *do* think it was madness. People either laugh at the likes of Martha Wilds or bring her pork belly in exchange for a spell. But Martha taught me how to bring my power out and I can show you how to reach yours. She also told me there's strength in numbers—something she never had. She said three is a magic number. Right now, I have two—me and Elizabeth—that's why we need *you*."

I folded my arms. "Need me for what?"

She smiled slyly. "So, we can be a force to be reckoned with. We're all orphans—my parents by pox, Elizabeth's mother died in jail 'cause of those girls you live with, and her stepfather cares not what she does—your parents, sold."

I bit my lips to hold back the tears threatening to swim in my eyes.

"Like I said," she continued, "you were the *talk* of the town, but we're all basically alone in the world where men—and women—think they can tell us what to do. They think they can beat us into submission. But Martha Wilds comes from a long line of folk women and she saw your power, Violet."

I shook my head. "I've never met this Martha Wilds— this is all nonsense."

Tammy grabbed my hand, and the heat almost burned me. "If a witch doesn't want to be seen, she'll be like a shadow and you'll walk right on by. Martha Wilds was there, and she saw *you*. She watched and studied you and she told me you have the power."

I pulled out of her grasp and scoffed. "If I have such *great* power, why haven't I noticed anything before? Why will I be getting a beating when I get home for not bringing enough kindling?"

Elizabeth leaned in toward me. "Tammy said sometimes it comes on by itself, *other times* you need a little help to get it working. I needed a little help, but now—now I just walked up on you in the woods and you didn't even hear me coming. I—well, I could've snuck right up on you and . . . *done something!*"

She sat up a little taller than before, and for the first time I really noticed her. She almost seemed to fill her dress. Elizabeth Prince was showing me she had a story to tell.

Tammy beamed. "If we are together, our magic could be unstoppable. No more switches or beatings. No more locking people up because some foolish girl pointed her finger. And maybe . . . you could find out where your mother and father are."

Tears stung my eyes and I hated the water pooling in front of Tammy, but if finding Mama and Papa meant working with this girl, I was all in.

I blinked away the tears. "What do I need to do?"

"You need to bring us a book. An unwritten book."

I shook my head. "I have no books!"

Elizabeth squeezed my hand. "You live with a pastor—*he* has unwritten books."

I thought about the blank journals Reverend Parris used

to write his sermons. He had talked about the cost of each book, how much it took from his family's needs. Could I steal from this family?

I felt a lightning bolt go through me. It was as if it were striking me for doubting the plan.

"Yes," I said breathlessly. "I can try."

Tammy nodded at me. "Martha told me if I could form a coven, we could use the book to right our wrongs."

I tilted my head in puzzlement. "Right our wrongs?"

Tammy grinned. "First we write our covenant, our agreement, and then we write our names. If we spill our blood on the empty pages, then the names of the people who need to be punished will appear, and magic will see that we are avenged."

CHAPTER SEVEN

They say hurt the children or we will do worse to you.
—TITUBA, FROM COURT TESTIMONY

I sat on that thought and imagined whose names might appear in this book. I knew there were plenty of people who deserved to be in such a book, but at that moment, the thought of truly inflicting dark punishment upon anyone made me shiver. I just wanted to be with Mama and Papa so badly that I nodded my head in agreement.

Tammy held out her hands, palms up, and Elizabeth and I each reached out. The moment our fingers touched, I felt Tammy's lightning course within me chasing out all my fears. "You get the book, Violet, and then we can get our familiars."

"Familiars?" I asked breathlessly.

"Familiars are witches' companions, animals who can do our bidding. They can be our eyes and ears: our spies. Next full moon, bring the book and something else—a tuft of fur, a snakeskin, or just a thought."

Elizabeth tittered and puffed her chest. "I will search the fence posts for gray wolf fur!"

Tammy beamed. "A wolf you shall have then, Elizabeth. And you, Violet?"

What would I have? Did I even believe?

I did have a small token I'd collected on my walks in the woods. When I found it, I couldn't pass it by and kept it carefully hidden under my mattress, safe from Betty's and Abigail's snooping. It was something that reminded me of the night spirits in the forests that Mama told me soared above the trees in her homeland.

"I–I have a tail feather from a raven. Would that work? Would I really be able to conjure up a raven to do my bidding?"

Tammy nodded and seemed pleased, as if she'd known all along what I would say. "Bring the book and the feather

56

at the next full moon and I promise you will see through a raven's eyes as it takes flight at your command."

I felt lighter than I had in months. It could all be nonsense and madness, but I felt as though I were taking control of my future. "I will get us a book even if I am whipped to the bone for it!"

I lifted my head to the sky and peered through the canopy.

When I am a witch, I will fly into the night sky and I will no longer be Violet Indian or Violet Somebody. I will command the stars to whisper my real name and they will point the way to Mama and Papa.

A smile lit my face, but then I saw Elizabeth, bedraggled and sunken in her oversized dress. There was no magic lighting up her face at the endless possibilities Tammy was promising.

My shadows reared and filled me with doubt. Was this all pretense? Was I a pawn in some twisted game of revenge?

After all, my mother had confessed to casting spells with Elizabeth's mother—who went to the grave denying such things.

Perhaps Elizabeth had gotten this Tammy girl to help her

strike out. Since Mama was gone, perhaps I was the one meant to suffer for her sins.

Although I had already given them my promise to get the book, I needed to taste a small bit of sorcery to give me the courage to do it.

"I need proof," I stated.

Tammy scowled. "Proof? Proof of what?"

I folded my arms across my chest. "Show me how to walk in the woods without making a sound. If you cannot, I will not risk my life stealing from the Parris house."

"Oh!" Elizabeth exclaimed. "I will show you."

I eyed her and found no pretense on her face, which was now lit up as if it were the sun itself.

Though perhaps a small thing, what Tammy and Elizabeth had done—sneaking up on me like that in a noisy wood filled with dry leaves and sticks that I'd spent hours upon hours in—well, it did seem *truly* magical to me.

No deer walked unheard, and no chipmunk ran quietly through the underbrush. If they could show me that magic, I would know I was not their target.

Though Tammy was the obvious leader in our newly

formed threesome, Elizabeth seemed to find the act of becoming *invisible* so satisfying, she seemed bursting to show me how to do it.

Elizabeth grabbed my hands and squeezed them tight. "Since my mother passed, my stepfather has made me feel as if I did not matter—as if I took up space he wished others would. He has no affection for myself or my brothers—I do believe he would be quite satisfied if we would simply disappear." She looked in my eyes. "So often I would love to do just that. Tammy has shown me what to do—how to become quiet—to slip into the background. It doesn't always work—"

"But it does, you've just done it," I said breathlessly, thinking of all the times I would love to have escaped notice in the Parris house.

Elizabeth's face opened like a morning glory at sunrise. "Ground your feet to the earth, feel as if you are sending roots deep into the soil, and then break free."

"Break free?" I asked. "How?"

Elizabeth took in a deep breath. "You ground yourself to the earth, sink all your weight into the forest floor, and then breathe in the air, forcing it to lift you on the breeze. Breathe in and be featherlight. Break away from your roots, be as light as a dandelion seed on the wind. Be invisible."

Tammy lifted her chin toward the sky and closed her eyes. "Be a thief," she added.

I watched Tammy as she took in three deep breaths. Her eyes snapped open as she threw her arms into the air and then took three silent steps toward me.

I took a deep breath and exhaled. My eyes locked on Tammy's. Could I really do this?

I imagined sending dark tendrils into the earth. I thought of Mama's world before they'd stolen her. I thought of birds gliding through the hot air high above the lush forest—I thought of becoming eiderdown—milkweed—dandelion seeds.

A small gasp left my lips as I felt an updraft lift through me and I took a step.

My feet seemed not to touch the forest floor. I reached my other boot forward and not a sound or snap answered. My eyes widened, and Tammy beamed. She took her own noiseless steps toward me and clasped my hands.

"You are a thief who walks on the wind," she whispered. "A thief with all the world for the taking."

CHAPTER EIGHT

I did see her set a wolf upon her to afflict her.
—TITUBA, FROM COURT TESTIMONY, 1692

 week later, I stood staring at the bookcase, staring at the reverend's book. Earlier this morning, I had seen Elizabeth in town, carrying a basket of eggs to sell. She did not greet me, but she simply tilted her chin slightly to the sky and gave me a questioning look. The moon was growing fuller with each passing day, but I could only give my head a tiny shake. Her face pinched in disappointment.

I wished I could tell Elizabeth that stealing the journal was an unnerving task. Had the job been assigned to her, she would likely be quaking in her boots. Simply passing the bookshelf as I set the table for meals filled me with such dread that my hands trembled as I filled the glasses with cider.

I held out my hand; the welt had turned from an angry red to a tender purple. After dinner last night, as I scrubbed the stains from the tablecloth, Reverend Parris switched my hand with one sharp strike and threatened worse if I continued to mar the linens.

I rolled my eyes to the heavens. The reverend could switch me all he wanted, but thankfully he could not read my mind and discover I was plotting an act of thievery. I walked over to the shelf and ran a shaking finger down the book's spine. There was only one spare journal sitting wedged between his Bibles and a handful of other books, and I knew his hawkish eyes would notice its absence as soon as it was gone.

If I could even work up the courage to take it.

Did I really dare?

The journal he currently used for his sermons was steadily filling up and it would only be a matter of days before he took the new one—the only one—from the shelf.

I had to act quickly, as it could be months before he purchased another.

But if that book were found in my possession, I feared I'd suffer more than just a whipping.

I wished I could talk to Tammy. Surely, a girl like that would know just how to steal a book without getting caught. I had to believe that Tammy would simply up and take it and walk right out of the house.

I looked down at the darkening bruise on the top of my hand, and a thought I'd been sitting on got up and raced around my head.

What if Tammy was a storyteller like Mama? She might be laughing this very moment about how she'd tricked me into stealing a book with her false promises of magic and finding my parents.

I touched the book and closed my eyes. I had so many questions about so many things.

But there was Elizabeth and Tammy teaching me to walk in the wood without so much as a branch snapping under foot. I felt as if I were as light as a chick and could have been carried off on the slightest breeze.

I certainly couldn't explain the power that coursed from Tammy's fingers.

I had felt that; it was as real as the heat lightning in a summer storm.

And there was Mama. In court she talked of Sarah Good with a yellow bird. Was that bird Sarah's *familiar*?

"Violet," Mistress Parris called out as she descended the stairs with Betty and Abigail trailing behind.

I blinked and rushed to the hearth to put as much distance between me and the shelf as possible.

They were wearing their visiting clothes. I looked down at their polished boots, praying my guilty thoughts weren't written on my face.

She picked up her Bible from the table and seemed to pay me no mind. "We are to call on the Walcotts on behalf of the reverend to inquire about their absence from the last four services. The reverend and Thomas will be home at five, so be sure to have dinner on the table when they arrive."

Her eyes drifted to the switch leaning on the wall next to me. "God frowns on carelessness, Violet. I expect the linens will not be stained tonight; your mother certainly never spilled a drop."

"Or let the porridge stick to the bottom of the pot," Betty added with a smirk.

I stared at her, wondering when she'd become so like her mother—so unlike the Betty I had known.

Abigail snickered at Betty's comment. "Or let the corner of the blanket hang off the mattress," she added, looking down her nose at me.

Mistress Parris sniffed as she made her way to the door. "Yes, it's a good thing your mother is not here to witness your sloppiness; she'd be greatly disappointed in you."

Disappointed? My stomach roiled with anger.

Betty glanced at me with wide eyes as heat seared my cheeks. Her mouth opened, and I thought she might say something, but then she looked away.

I *had* been making small acts of defiance since we got back from Gloucester—a blanket not properly tucked in; porridge left on the hearth a minute too long—nothing so grave that it should get me whipped. But to hear her say it was a good thing Mama wasn't here cut me to the quick.

Would Mama be disappointed in me? I felt the shadows I carried within me send their tendrils deeper inside my body and I wondered if there was any light left in me at all.

"Mistress Parris?"

Mistress Parris turned from the page she'd opened in her Bible. "Yes, Violet?"

"I do not think my mother would be disappointed in me, and I am sorry she is not here to prove you wrong."

Mistress Parris's eyes widened for a second before narrowing into two indignant slits. "I disagree," she said curtly, and I cursed my bravado as my legs turned to churned butter. "And it is the reverend who is the sole judge of the quality of your work. I will see that he discusses his opinions with you this evening."

I bowed my head to keep from melting under the heat of her gaze. While Mistress Parris was not one to shout, her quiet anger was as powerful as Tammy's bottled lightning.

"Let us go, girls, we have God's work to do."

"Why do *we* have to go?" Abigail groaned. "This has none to do with us."

I glanced up in time to see Mistress Parris swat Abigail

across the cheek with the back of her gloved hand. "Because the reverend wants us to impress upon them the harm that can come from not attending services and obeying God's will. Do you have any other questions, Abigail? Perhaps you have something you'd like to add, Betty?"

The girls shook their heads, and Mistress Parris clutched her Bible to her breast. The three of them walked past me as if I were a phantom, invisible to their eyes. As soon as the door shut, I suddenly knew what I would do.

This phantom would take the journal, and the girls who had been responsible for Mama being thrown in prison, *they* would feel the switch tonight. Tonight, stained linens would be the last thing on the reverend's mind, and I would be one step closer to finding Mama and Papa.

I walked to the window and watched the three women make their way down the dusty road. Once out of sight, I turned and stepped slowly toward the shelf. My resolve wavered the closer I got, but I willed myself to keep moving.

"Be like Tammy," I whispered, my eyes focused on the book. "Be strong so you take control of your life."

With a trembling hand I reached for the journal. I wasn't

sure when the reverend would notice it was gone. I ripped four pages out and then hurriedly wrapped the book in an oilcloth and raced toward the woods to hide it, praying my plan would work.

It had to.

My life depended on it.

CHAPTER NINE

t five o'clock sharp, Reverend Parris and Thomas entered the house. I had taken extra care cooking and seasoning the stew. Each spoon lay perfectly straight on the carefully folded napkins, and even though my body had felt like it could shake into pieces, not a drop of cider marred the white table linen.

The reverend did a quick assessment of the main room. Abigail and Betty had just put their stitching away and were making their way to the table as Mistress Parris was hastily folding her apron. It took every ounce of self-control to not glance at the bookshelf, and I slowly exhaled when his attention settled on his wife.

"What word do you have from the Walcotts, Mrs. Parris? Shall I expect them for this Sunday's worship?"

She sniffed as we all took our places at the table. "Apparently, the gout has struck Mr. Walcott and Mrs. Walcott insists she can't leave him alone to attend worship all day. I must say Mr. Walcott did not seem much afflicted to me, but I delivered your note of warning that should they remain away, litigation may be taken. I pray they will have a change of heart."

"*Change of heart?*" he asked, one eyebrow rising in puzzlement.

She smiled weakly and dipped a ladle into the stew. "I did not secure a promise they would be in attendance for your next service."

His nostrils flared. "Did you impress upon them the importance of attending worship? Did you speak of God's anger to see their empty seats week after week?"

"I did my best, but you know my words do not carry the same weight as yours."

She filled the bowl, avoiding his steely gaze. "But Mr. Walcott did impress upon me that he has had many visitors

to his home and all have said that attendance for worship is down. He said his empty seat would be . . . hard to pick out amongst all the others."

The reverend slammed his palms on the table, and cider spilled from the cups. Mistress Parris flinched, and a large blob of stew splashed onto the white linen cloth.

"Careless woman, look what you've done!" he boomed, his gaunt face reddening.

Thomas, Betty, Abigail, and I all froze as the reverend rose swiftly and stalked toward Mistress Parris. It was no secret the reverend had never been a well-liked man and the town's opinion of him was made all the worse by his part in the witch trials. It was also no secret that doing God's work had not spared him from having a fiery temper.

He snatched the ladle from her hand and flung it across the room, where it clattered against the hearth. "Why do I bother to send you as a messenger of the Lord if you cannot impress upon a simpleton such as Mr. Walcott that those who care not for me should still be attending worship!"

He turned and grabbed his journal from the desk. Breathing heavily, he looked toward Betty. "Fetch the ladle

and see that you prove to be less clumsy than your mother and our useless servant."

"Yes, Father." Betty rose slowly from the table and then shooed away the dog, who was licking the ladle clean. As she rinsed the ladle in a bowl of water, the reverend walked back to his place and set the journal next to his napkin. By the time Betty came back to the table, the reverend's breathing had slowed, and he spoke matter-of-factly as if he had not just behaved in a most unholy manner.

"I have decided to change the topic of Sunday's sermon to stress upon the community the importance of worship no matter the feelings for who is leading it. And what have I done that was so grievous? Ask for a decent salary? Ask for the kindling that is stipulated in my contract? When was the last time someone had even a stick to spare for the man who speaks for God?"

He smiled coolly, gesturing to the table. "At least I can be thankful for this meal to share with my family."

The reverend folded his hands together and we bowed our heads. "We thank thee our Lord for this bounty and pray that the Walcotts come back to our fold. I beseech

You to also guide the Tarbell, Nurse, and Lewis families back into Your good graces, so we may see them at services as well. And lastly, we thank You, Lord, that You have seen fit to secure our Thomas an apprenticeship with Reverend Increase Mather. Amen."

Mistress Parris's head popped up in surprise and she reached a hand to her son's arm. "Oh, that is blessed news! Our Thomas is to be a minister, too!"

Thomas nodded, but his face did not mirror her obvious pleasure. Over the years, the reverend had pushed pencils and books on his son, but it was Betty who was more interested in the written word. Seeing her curious about what the marks on the pages of his Bible were, the reverend had indulged her and educated her alongside her brother until Betty told some of her friends. As word spread, the reverend chastised her for having a loose tongue and ended her lessons, telling her she should concentrate on "women's work."

It was because of Betty that Abigail and I could write our names.

When her parents were out of the house, Betty would

teach us the letters of our names in the ashes or with a stick in the dirt out in the yard. Eventually, Betty acquired a slate that she kept hidden from her parents, but even Mama had learned to write a capital *T* in white chalk.

But I knew Thomas's heart was not found in the pages of a book, as he seemed to prefer the feel of a hammer in hand, often working side by side with Papa. They never talked much, but Thomas—unlike the reverend—appeared to prefer the same quiet Papa did.

"It is fortunate I have a spare book for you to gather your thoughts, Thomas. I will implore the town to give heartily at the next service so I can purchase a new one for myself."

My bottom lip quivered as the reverend's words sunk in.

Would the reverend look to the shelf now? Would he see what was missing? And if he did, would I be able to keep my head and let my plan come to fruition?

CHAPTER TEN

We ride upon sticks and are there presently.
—Tituba, from court testimony

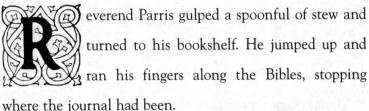everend Parris gulped a spoonful of stew and turned to his bookshelf. He jumped up and ran his fingers along the Bibles, stopping where the journal had been.

"Have you seen the book, the new one I was able to purchase with the tithings last month?"

Mistress Parris shook her head, the candle flickering in her questioning eyes.

Reverend Parris yanked books out before he hastily pushed them back in. "Where is the book? It was five shillings!"

"I know not, Father." Mistress stood up. "Violet, were you tending to the shelves?"

"I . . ." I paused to remember the words I'd practiced all day should this very question be asked of me. "I have only worked on the stew and bread baking today, Mistress. And I have been told not to touch the reverend's things."

She pursed her lips. "Betty? Abigail? Have you been at Father's books?"

"No!" Betty squeaked, pulling at the end of her braid nervously, while Abigail shook her head vigorously.

"Well, the book did not get up and walk away on its own!" barked the reverend. "Thomas, what do you know of it?"

Thomas's eyes were as wide as everyone else's. The reverend was in a fury, and he knew there would be harsh punishment. "I know nothing, Father. Until we met with Reverend Mather today, I had no need of such things."

"Surely, it has simply been misplaced, Father," Mistress said, rushing to the shelf. "It must be right in front of us." She leaned over and began to scour the lower shelves.

Reverend Parris stood before us, his face the color of

maple leaves in the fall. "The book cost *five* shillings. *Five!*"
One by one, he glared at us all. "Stand!"

Mistress put her hand on the reverend's arm. "Samuel, it is *just* a book."

"*Five. Shillings,*" he growled. "It took months to save up enough to finally buy this."

I stood, head held high.

I am strong like Tammy. I have lightning in my blood. I am strong like Tammy. I have lightning in my blood.

The reverend studied our faces. "Who would covet such a book?"

When his gray eyes met mine, I lifted my chin and met his gaze. I held my breath, and when he moved on to Betty, I wished I were a scarecrow with a pole against my back as it took all my concentration to keep myself from sinking to the floor.

"Betty," he said softly, "why do you not meet my gaze? Have you taken the book?"

From the corners of my eyes I saw her cheeks redden. "No, Father."

"It shall be the worse for you if you do not tell the truth."

She shook her head but still did not look up. "I have not taken your book, Father."

"Then you shall not mind if I search your things?"

"You may search it all, Father. I have nothing to hide." She licked her lips and swallowed.

Her words held such conviction that I feared Reverend Parris might turn his attention back to me, but before that worry could even take root in my head, Abigail let out a gasp.

"Don't, Reverend!" she blubbered. "Don't go up there, I beg you."

He slapped his hands together with a sharp crack. "*Thieves!* Thieves under my own roof."

He turned and stalked up the stairs.

Betty stood wild-eyed, watching him go. "*It was a bluff,*" she hissed to Abigail. "And because of you—!"

"*Bluff?* How do you even dare to bluff when we . . . ?" Abigail collapsed in her chair, sobbing. "We are done for."

Mistress Parris walked slowly to her own chair and lowered herself down, her face as blank as the slate hidden under Betty and Abigail's mattress. "What mischief now, Betty?" she asked wearily.

What mischief indeed.

While Mistress Parris and the girls had been visiting the Walcotts, I discovered I was not the only one who was making mischief, and I braced myself for the hurricane that was about to unleash itself inside this house.

Three years ago, Betty had taken a slate and chalk from the meetinghouse. The slate belonged to Jonathon Brattle but Betty was determined to continue her lessons with or without her father's blessings. Abigail and I thought she was being scandalous, but Betty emphasized how unfair it was that Thomas, who barely concentrated during lessons, would continue to learn to read and write and she was forced to practice stitchery.

It was hard to argue her point, and using that slate to learn to write was far more exciting than using a stick in the dirt or a finger in the ashes.

It was also another one of the secrets we girls shared. I still remember the day I nervously showed Mama my name written on that slate while Betty, the proud teacher, stood by my side.

Mama had marveled at it. "That's *your* name? Those scribbles say *Violet*? And you wrote that yourself?"

I nodded, and I could see from her face that her heart swelled with pride. "My baby, learning to write?"

Tears swam in her dark brown eyes and she hugged me. "I never would have thought, but don't be showing this to the reverend or the mistress!"

Betty grabbed the slate and in a flash my hard work was gone. "I can teach you how to write your name, too, Mama Tituba." She drew a *T*, and Mama reached out and traced a finger along the two lines.

"Well, that was easy enough," Mama said, but as Betty wrote the rest of her name, Mama shook her head. "What's this called?" she asked, pointing to the first letter.

"Tee! Tee for Tituba."

Mama traced it again and then folded her arms across her chest. "I think *Tee* is enough for me. I'll leave the learning to you smart girls."

At that moment I was thankful Betty had stolen the slate, and until today I believed Betty's act of thievery had been an isolated one. But when I'd lifted the mattress to place the four sheets of paper I'd ripped from the book and on which I had written their names, my jaw dropped. Shell beads, poppets, and even a pearl-white comb were stashed alongside the slate and chalk.

Some of these things I imagine could have been left behind in the meetinghouse and picked up by the girls, but there were also several thimbles, a hornbook, and a pencil that I knew did not belong to the Parrises.

Being the daughter and the niece of the town's minister, Betty and Abigail were often visiting families, and I wondered whether they used these opportunities to come away with trinkets and baubles. I'd left the stolen goods where they were and then lowered the mattress, leaving a small corner of the page I'd ripped from the book barely sticking out. I was sure the girls would not notice, but I knew the reverend would.

Seeing their stolen treasures had chased away some of the unease I felt about setting the girls up for a fall, but despite their coldness to me over the last year, I took no pleasure knowing what was to come.

"Violet, clear the table and then bring in some more kindling," Mistress said quietly. "I feel it might get a bit chilly tonight."

I had already gathered plenty of kindling and the

evening was warm, but I nodded. "Yes, Mistress. I feel a chill as well."

She stared straight ahead, her face drawn and weary, and I supposed she was bracing herself for that storm about to boil over onto the girls. "Thomas, go to the Hubbards' and inquire if they have any use for you. I recall Mrs. Hubbard stating that her husband's hands have arthritis and their barn needs some repair. I am thinking you might be able to earn some coins to help pay for a new book."

Thomas left swiftly, surely thankful to be out of the house before his father descended the stairs. I rose and quickly cleared the table, anxious to be gone myself. Abigail was still sobbing, albeit gently, and Betty sat with her hands folded neatly on the table, looking for all the world to be at peace with her fate.

While Betty and Abigail were about to be hit with gale-force winds—their storm had left me free to retrieve the book I'd wrapped in a cloth and hidden at the edge of the woods. In one night, I'd be with my new *sisters*, and I would write my name once again.

"*Mistress Parris!*" the reverend boomed from upstairs.

We all, even Betty, jumped clear out of our skin at the rage that shook the house.

"Bring the girls upstairs at once! *And have Betty bring the crop.*"

My heart pounded, and Abigail's head shot up, her red-rimmed eyes nearly popping from her head. A long, terrified yelp rose from her throat.

Mistress Parris bowed her head and took a deep breath as she rose. "You heard the reverend, Betty, get the crop."

Betty's body went rigid and Abigail let out a long howl not unlike the day she said she was first bewitched.

Visibly shaking, Betty ran to her mother and clung to her arm. "Mother, no. Don't let him." She ran to the hearth and took hold of the switch. "Tell him to hit us harder, tell him to use all his might, but don't let him use the crop."

"Fetch it now," Mistress Parris said, with a chill in her voice.

"*Make haste!*" the reverend yelled from upstairs.

"Quickly!" Mistress implored. "Or it shall be worse for the wait."

"This is *your* doing!" Abigail shrieked to Betty. "I never

would have taken *any* of those things had you not implored me to."

"*Things?*" Mistress whispered. "There is more to this than just . . . a book?"

I could recall only one time when the reverend had used the crop to dole out a punishment. My papa had been hired by a sea captain to work on some loose ship boards and he dropped a hammer into the bay while working on the pier.

A switch could deliver a welt, but a crop could break you. It was just then that I remembered Papa used to be more like Mama. He used to laugh. How could I have forgotten that Papa used to laugh?

"Violet, go now and take your time returning."

I ran from the table and raced out the door, shutting it loudly behind me. I picked up the basket from the front stoop and hurried toward the woods, wondering if Abigail's wails could be heard from as far away as Mama's old jail cell in Boston, and if Papa had found his laugh again wherever he was.

CHAPTER ELEVEN

s I headed down the path through the Putnams' hayfield, my skin felt cool and clammy despite the warm evening. Come Sabbath, Betty and Abigail would wish to be lying in bed, but as part of their punishment I knew they would have to sit all day on the raw skin and bruises they were about to receive.

I had set this in motion, but I tried to comfort myself, knowing that Betty and Abigail deserved what was coming to them. Not only had they been stealing from the townspeople, but they had never truly been punished for what they did to Mama—or Mrs. Prince or any of the other people that died because of them.

Unless they truly had been afflicted.

I shook my head.

What was true?

What were lies?

I was sure Mama would never have hurt anyone like they claimed.

Like Mama claimed, too—until she recanted. But did having powers mean you had to do bad things? Or could powers be used to help a person like I was trying to help myself?

How could I ever be sure, when Mama was too far away to ask?

In frustration, I kicked a rock from my path, stirring up a cloud of dust. Only one more night until the full moon, and I was praying that book would help me find the answers I was looking for.

A hearty laugh up ahead stopped me in my tracks. There—in the spot just inside the edge of the woods and twenty steps from the path where I had hidden the book—stood Thomas Parris.

My heart jumped like a rabbit a breath away from a hound's mouth. Had he seen me hide the book when I thought he was out with his father? Did he know?

Had all the trouble I'd stirred up been for nothing?

I picked up my pace until I heard another laugh—a girl's laugh.

I froze.

Thomas was not alone.

I slowed my steps, squinting to see who was with him.

Hands reached up to run through his hair, and he wrapped his arms around a girl, lifting her up in the air and then leaning in to plant a kiss on her lips as soon as her feet touched the ground.

"Why, Thomas Parris, what would your father say if he could see you now?"

"He'd say, '*Thomas Parris, get me the crop!*'"

"Am I worth the crop, Thomas Parris?" she cooed.

"*You* are worth a *branding*."

He leaned in again and heat rose up through my whole body. I was rooted to the spot, terrified to move lest they see me, and yet, I couldn't look away. In the past, Betty and Abigail and I had spent hours talking about what kisses might be like and we'd even practiced on the back of our hands. But I had never even seen anyone, not even my parents, kiss. We knew people did it, though; more than a few men and women had spent a day in the stocks for such displays of public affection.

I was gobsmacked that Thomas could be so shameless where anyone could stumble upon him, but I had recognized the girl's voice as soon as she spoke.

Instead of visiting the Hubbards to inquire about work, Thomas Parris was risking everything by standing at the edge of the woods kissing Tammy Younger. Upon seeing them, my first instinct was to run back to the house, but an idea took hold.

Tammy Younger had no doubt cast some spell on Thomas Parris to make him behave this way, but I knew I could use his indiscretion to my advantage. And though I wasn't a full-fledged witch yet—we'd not finalized a covenant with our names signed in the book—Tammy and Elizabeth had shown me I could weave some magic of my own.

The day I had promised to break the Lord's commandment and steal the reverend's book, I had walked on the wind.

I had also felt Tammy's power, but in the back of my mind, I thought that some people were just like that—potent and crackling with energy. Betty and Abigail, for instance, were like night and day, with Betty leading the day and Abigail living in her shadow. And it would not have been a stretch to say Reverend Parris or Sheriff Corwin or even maybe Mama had some of that bottled lightning coursing through their veins. I just thought perhaps Tammy had more of it in her than most.

Though the dirt path to the woods was generally a quiet one, I wanted to surprise Thomas *and* Tammy. I needed to. I needed to show Tammy that the power was not all hers. While walking through the woods, I'd been practicing what Elizabeth had taught me. I felt light as air as I snuck up on a suckling fawn and its mother. Another time, a telltale snap cracked under my feet and sent chipmunks scattering away. Right now, I needed nothing to go wrong.

I breathed in through my nose and closed my eyes. I imagined myself a sturdy weed with a taproot deep in the ground. I imagined growing a yellow flower and then all the water and weight leaving me until I was a single dandelion seed—airy, delicate, noiseless. I exhaled, feeling the weight leave my body and rise above me. My heavy boots seemed made of clouds. I breathed in again, then exhaled and became a piece of goose down on the wind.

I opened my eyes and my usually heavy steps made their way silently along the path, and I stirred up not a mote of dust.

Magic.

My magic.

I neared them quickly, quietly. Thomas and Tammy clung to each other still, and I forged ahead despite feeling sick watching them hanging on each other so—their lips locked together.

I was practically upon them when I stopped, stamped a foot on the ground to reclaim my weight, and felt gleeful as they looked up in shock.

"*Thomas Parris?*" I gasped in mock surprise. "What pray thee *are* you doing?"

Thomas flew away from Tammy, his wet mouth open and trembling like a fish on a hook pier. "Violet! I . . ."

Tammy giggled and stepped closer to him, wrapping her arm in his. "Who's your friend, Thomas?" She winked at me as he tore himself away from her—his head down and shoulders hunched.

"Stop it, Tammy!" he scolded in a quiet voice. "This is Violet; she works in my house."

"I recall hearing about this Violet Indian, your slave girl, in town," Tammy said, matter-of-fact.

She winked at me again, and I knew she was playing along with my ruse. But I couldn't help but wonder: Does she not realize that her harsh words sting and cut so close to the bone?

"Yes. I. Am. And my mistress, his *mother*, sent me to the wood to get kindling."

Tammy shrugged and smiled at me, but her smile didn't fill me with light. I was not at all feeling sisterly toward her, but perhaps this was part of her act.

"Thomas," I said, "I thought you were going to the Hubbards'. Imagine my shock to see you here with . . . *this*." I pursed my lips and lowered my chin.

There was no pretense now; I was embarrassed finding him and Tammy together, but I prayed Thomas Parris was not only shamed, but scared.

He looked at me finally, and his frightened eyes were none

too different from that of Abigail's as she'd sat at the table not so long ago. I could see the wheels turning in his head—jumping forward to a future in the stocks and what that would mean for his father's already shaky reputation in the village. What it would mean for his future. Perhaps he was even thinking of how he had just joked about getting beaten with the riding crop and how it might become a reality.

Perhaps he was thinking those stolen kisses were not such a bargain anymore or that a beating at home might be better than being displayed in front of the whole town.

"It's not—it's not what it looks like, Violet."

Tammy laughed and took kitten steps toward him. "Oh," she purred, "it is exactly what it looks, Thomas Parris. And were you not bragging a minute ago I was worth a branding?" She giggled and tried to fall into his arms, but he pushed her away.

"Stop it!" he yelled. "Do you not see the gravity in this?"

Tears welled in his eyes, but she simply put her fingers to her lips and then reached toward Thomas's face. "What great weight is a simple kiss?"

He danced back out of her reach, staring at her with new

eyes and shook his head. It was obvious Thomas was finally realizing the true *gravity* of playing along with Tammy Younger's rules, rules that did not align with his father's or the town's—and perhaps no one's but Tammy's.

I stepped toward him and laid a gentle hand on his arm. "You need not fear me, Thomas. I will not tell your secret. There have been people in the stocks for doing just this or more. You are not alone in this indiscretion and I do not condemn you."

He wept while Tammy scoffed. "Ours is a true love, Thomas, you've said as much."

"Betty and Abigail are getting the crop tonight," I continued. "Your father is in a dark place and I recommend you visit the Hubbards' at haste."

He nodded and without another word raced toward town.

As soon as he was out of earshot, I laid into Tammy. "How long has this been going on? How long have you been *corrupting* Thomas Parris?"

CHAPTER TWELVE

orrupting, Thomas? That is laughable. Thomas Parris is a willing and able partner."

I waved my hands in the air. "Be that as it may—how are you two here on the very spot where I've—"

She smiled slyly. "Hidden the book?"

She ran a few paces back and plucked the fabric-wrapped package from a new hiding spot, holding it over her head and dancing around the path. "I've watched you every day from the woods—wishing and waiting for you to succeed, and in that period . . . I have encountered Thomas Parris on many occasions. Did you know he hates his father and misses yours?"

My lips pulled inward. She said this so matter-of-factly, as if not even considering how deeply felt my father's loss was to *me*.

"He has no interest in becoming a preacher, and from the way he kisses me, he has not heard a higher calling."

She stretched the book toward me, and I took it from her, blushing.

"So, you have been watching me?" I asked.

"Every day."

"And what of Elizabeth?"

"Elizabeth is here as well."

Leaves shifted under foot as Elizabeth came forward from the shadows. Her face flushed a deeper red than mine.

"A spectacle, was it not?" I asked, hoping for some comradery in my misery.

Elizabeth buried her face in her hands. "Oh, to stand in silence and watch what marrieds do . . . I cannot even imagine how I survived it."

Tammy rolled her eyes. "Be that a lesson to you, girls, no matter what they say at services, people *like* to kiss. They just can't be caught doing it."

Elizabeth's eyes widened, and Tammy threw back her head with a howl.

"It's *fine* to kiss. Up in Gloucester they care not—"

"We are not in Gloucester!" I shrieked. "I have two girls at home taking a savage beating because we are *not* in Gloucester and I have stolen and I have been deceitful. *They* are paying a very hefty price."

Tammy's eyes widened. "Am I supposed to be sorry for that? For them?" She folded her arms across her chest. "Because I am not. I have learned that one must look out for oneself, and I dare say it is about *time* someone thrashed those brats within an inch of their lives for all the trouble they wrought. How you can have an ounce of sympathy for them is beyond my wildest imaginings."

"If you knew the reverend like I do—like Thomas does— you might feel *something* for them."

Tammy scoffed. "Need I remind you that Elizabeth's mother is *dead* because of them."

I looked to Elizabeth, her bottom lip quivering. Tears caught in her pale lashes and she bowed her head.

"So many are dead, and you sleep without a mother or father in that cold, barren house because of those girls." Tammy stared at me, her eyes two hard stones. "No, I have not an ounce of pity in my heart for them and nor should you."

In my own heart I knew Tammy was likely right. Betty and Abigail probably did not deserve my pity, but perhaps a small corner of my soul had not been so consumed with blackness, because I *did* pity them. Despite all they had done, my stomach was in knots thinking about the beating they were getting—because of me.

I also knew that to condemn them fully would be to condemn my mother as well. Mama could have confessed without accusing others. If Mama had done that and not talked of flying in the woods, might the whole thing have ended then and there and not over a hundred and fifty accused and twenty people dead? Betty and Abigail had started things, but Mama made them take off like a wildfire in the dry August heat.

Oh, I wished Mama were here to tell me all that really happened.

I felt the weight of the book in my hand. When I write my name in its pages, will I still be able to feel compassion—even for those who perhaps deserved none? It was dark magic we would be invoking—dark magic full of revenge.

Could I really go through with this?

"I feel you wavering, Violet *Somebody*," Tammy said, her voice softer than before. "We *need* you and you need us. You sleep alone in a cold house," she repeated. "And if you are ever to find your parents, *this* . . ." She tapped the book. "This is how you do it."

I nodded. I would have no peace for the rest of my life if I couldn't find Mama and have her tell me what really happened. I handed the book to her. "Take this back to Elizabeth's. My nerves could not stand to have it anywhere near the Parris house."

"I will keep it tucked away safe in the barn," Tammy said. "Tomorrow the moon is full. Wrap your fur or feather or *wish* in a bundle with an egg."

I looked to her. "An *egg*?"

"For our familiars to be born from," Elizabeth whispered, her eyes darting about the woods nervously.

"Elizabeth Prince, steady yourself!" Tammy exclaimed. "You are about to become a witch!"

Elizabeth wrung her hands and looked back at us. "Are we to really do this?" She gathered us close. "Are we really to become full-fledged *witches* tomorrow evening?"

Tammy smiled. "Tomorrow we harness the power of three. Tomorrow we become *women*."

Elizabeth stood tall, her face glowing. "Women to be *reckoned* with."

I looked up through the branches at the darkening sky. Tomorrow, I would wrap a raven feather in a bundle with an egg. I'd been mesmerized by my mother's ability to see the future in the contents of an egg, and now I was a girl ready to cast her own spells on the world.

I smiled at Tammy and Elizabeth. "We will be women to be reckoned with, and women who can *fly*."

CHAPTER THIRTEEN

I spent much of the next day tending to Betty's and Abigail's wounds. The reverend had taken the Bible to heart and *not* spared the rod. I was horrified by his viciousness as I gently dabbed their cuts with honey.

I was also plagued with guilt that I had brought this upon them. Their acts of thievery would have gone unnoticed had I not slipped them into my new story.

Tammy's words echoed.

Elizabeth's mother is dead. Her stepfather cares not for her.

You sleep without a mother or a father, as they were sold.

It would be easy to think they deserved the red and blue lines across their buttocks—the raw and bleeding welts—but it was too much. I could not expel the guilt from my heart.

I knew Tammy would mock me for even feeling the slightest remorse, but I almost wanted—no, *expected*—Betty and Abigail to accuse me of forging those pages with their names and placing them under the mattress. It was obvious they had guessed what I had done—that I had set them up for a fall.

But there were no questions nor fingers pointed my way.

They remained silent, save for Abigail's soft weeping. Surely, they knew I was responsible, and I racked my head as to why they hadn't turned on me.

When I brought their plates up for dinner, I offered the hundredth apology in my head as the words stuck in my throat.

Perhaps, when I sign the book tonight, I can turn back time and do it all over differently, but I couldn't understand why their silence cut me more than their usual ugly remarks.

I still had to get out of the house later and that was yet another problem. It seemed my problems were piling up all

around me. I could walk along a path without making a sound, but how could I get past a sleeping dog or silence a noisy front door? What excuse could I give if I were caught out of the house?

I walked to the window and stared out to the woods from the diamond-shaped panes in time to see a figure striding toward the house.

Thomas.

His deliberate steps marked urgency, and I wondered what news he would bring.

The door opened and slammed, and my breath quickened.

"Mother!" he cried.

I stood at the top of the stairs but could make nothing of their hushed conversation.

"Violet," Mistress Parris called. "Come down at once!"

Abigail moaned from the bed and Betty shushed her, reaching out an arm to wrap around her.

"I'll be back soon," I said, not expecting an answer. "And I am *truly* sorry," I choked out for the first time aloud.

I raced down the stairs not wanting to anger Mistress Parris with tardiness. Feelings were raw in the house and I

did not want to push things further.

Mistress Parris stood by the table, hands on her hips. She turned to Thomas. "Why again do they need Violet? There seems no need for this. The girls need tending."

Thomas caught my eye briefly and then turned to his mother. "All I know, I was in town and Elizabeth Prince's stepfather, Mr. Osborne, beckoned me. He said their cow was in hard labor and that Tituba knew a remedy for such things. He hoped Violet might also know of it—she might have learned how to help from her mother. He'd heard it worked wonders, and he said he would pay coins if she could save his calf."

My mind searched for a conversation with Mama about birthing calves and came up with none. My mother was skilled in many things—but I could not remember her talking of animals and their care.

"Violet, you can help, right?" Thomas asked. "Elizabeth was sure you could. She asked for you to come immediately."

He stared me down and I understood. Tammy was using Thomas Parris so I could be free for the evening—so I could be out in the woods with nobody wondering where I

was. That kiss I witnessed was coming back to haunt him, making him do our bidding.

I wanted to smile but I saw Mistress Parris's face—saw the doubt in her eyes.

"Mama did say there were herbs that help with labor."

"*What* herbs, Violet?" she asked, eyes narrowed.

My mind raced for some birthing talk to remember. "Trillium. It helps with the contractions."

She turned to Thomas. "How many coins did Mr. Osborne say she could fetch?"

He shook his head. "He said not."

Mistress strode to the hearth. "You need a writing book, Thomas. We must take what we can get. Violet, can you get this *trillium?*"

I nodded vigorously. "I have spied some, Mistress, in the woods, and I recall having heard my mother speak of its effectiveness, but birthing can be a long process."

Thomas and I exchanged looks, and I wondered what Tammy had said to persuade him to get me out of the house tonight.

Perhaps it was the promise of another kiss.

Mistress looked at the chickens boiling in the pot over the fire. "Go, Violet, and be sure not to leave until you are paid."

I nodded and raced to my room for my traveling cap. I tucked my hair under and then snatched the black raven feather I had slid under my mattress. I gently took the quill and placed it in my apron pocket. I took the egg I had set aside under my pillow and pocketed that as well.

"I hope the birthing goes quickly, Mistress," I said, heading for the door. "I do not want to leave the girls for long."

Mistress hung her head, looking like she'd aged ten years just this evening. "I will tend to the girls. Just be sure you do not come home without the coins."

Once the door was shut behind me, I raced to the woods, cradling the egg in my hand. I took no measures to mask my steps as I flew through the trees in this evening, already ablaze by the full, white, magical moon.

CHAPTER FOURTEEN

I forged on, deeper and deeper, my breath labored, until I approached the spot I'd first met Tammy Younger. The stream only murmured now without the melted snow to fill it out, but the soft babble soothed my frayed nerves.

A glow caught my eye in the distance, and I saw it was a small fire.

My breath caught in my chest.

Would all I'd been promised—all I'd hoped—come true?

I slowed my steps as I neared the spot we'd chosen. A large oak had come down past winter, leaving an opening in the forest canopy for the moon to shine down. Elizabeth was poking a fiery log with a stick, while Tammy walked in circles around her.

Many of those who confessed to witchcraft had told of similar scenes—meetings out in the woods under the cover of night. Despite Tammy's assurance that people paid no mind to "folk women," I prayed I would not be confessing this evening's doings to Sheriff Corwin or Reverend Parris anytime in the future.

I had half a mind to turn and walk away, but I thought of that cold house I resided in. I thought of all the things I wanted but could never get on my own.

"I'm here," I said softly.

Elizabeth jumped up and Tammy turned to me, smiling triumphantly.

Tammy stretched out her arms and I walked slowly into them. "I knew you'd come."

I let her embrace me, and her bear hug made it clear she was truly afraid I might not show.

"Thomas did his part," I said.

Elizabeth danced around the fire with giddiness. "I'm so nervous," she tittered. "And excited! Will we really be able to make magic?"

Tammy's eyes glowed. "We will, and we'd best make haste

before someone comes looking for Violet and a newborn calf."

"We do have a cow in labor, so it wasn't really lying," Elizabeth stated. "I may be doing *witchy* things, but I do not want to offend the Lord any more than I have to by telling another lie."

"We are *folk women*," Tammy fired back.

"What of the coins, though?" I asked nervously. "Thomas promised the mistress I would receive coins for my help. I fear if I come back empty-handed she will make noise at Elizabeth's house and we will be exposed."

Tammy reached into her pocket. "I have but one—"

"No, *I* had but one!" Elizabeth said. "She took it from me; I had earned it for selling eggs this last year."

Tammy rolled her eyes. "Perhaps we can find a way to multiply it."

Elizabeth snatched it from her fingers, grinning madly. "Could we? Could we really?"

"I am *determined* to make it happen," Tammy said, grabbing it back. "Let us start."

"Should—should we get naked?" Elizabeth whispered.

"Would that help work the magic?"

Tammy laughed as I gasped.

"Only if you want to, Elizabeth Prince. I, for one, plan on becoming a witch, pardon—a folk woman—with my dress on and save my naked *flesh* for Thomas Parris."

"Oh, you are shameless!" Elizabeth squeaked.

"Says the person about to dance in the wood *frockless!*" I exclaimed, feeling blood rush to my face.

Elizabeth shrugged. "I am new to this witchery, folk-women business—I don't know the rules. It just *seemed* like getting naked might help. People did talk of that during the trials."

Tammy looked down her nose at Elizabeth. "*We* are harnessing the magic of the full moon; therefore, *we* make the rules."

"Well," Elizabeth sniffed, "if we are to make the rules, I declare we keep our dresses on, but remove our caps." She tossed her cap into the fire and shook out her long brown hair, giggling all the while. "I feel so scandalous!"

Tammy cocked her head and laughed. "I like the way you are thinking, Elizabeth Prince. I may have had my doubts about you, but you have the makings of a fine witchy folk woman!" She tossed her own cap into the fire, and they both looked to me as black smoke stung my nose.

"Oh no!" I shook my head. "I can't. If I come home without my cap there will be whipping, and given the number of whippings in the house of late, I do not want to draw attention to myself."

Elizabeth smirked. "Tell Mistress Parris the cow ate it!"

Tammy gawked at Elizabeth as fresh laughter filled the wood.

"Very well!" I took my cap off and plopped it on the glowing embers.

"Look at them burn," Tammy said, her chest rising fast. "We have just shed our old skins like snakes, and we are about to be reborn. Now let us dig a hole, bury our bundles, and see what drags itself out from the earth."

Tammy bent over a basket beside the fire and took out a small hand shovel. "We'll take turns digging—each one scoop and then we put the book and our bundles in."

"How deep should we dig?" I asked.

Tammy cleared a circle on the forest floor with her feet.

She examined it, and then brushed more debris away. She held out a boot and drew a circle as big as a wagon wheel in the dirt with its heel. "Because our brave Elizabeth wishes to command a wolf—very deep!"

"Oh no!" Elizabeth said. "I was thinking but a *tiny* wolf—a pup. The fur I pulled from the fence post surrounding the chicken yard seemed but soft baby fur."

Tammy handed her the shovel. "Dig deep; we do not know how big it will be when it comes."

"If it comes," she muttered.

Tammy squeezed her wrist. "It will come!"

Elizabeth pulled her arm away and then knelt on the forest floor. "For my wolf, then," she said, breaking the ground with the shovel.

We each took turns and sweat broke out on my forehead as I twisted the shovel to dig out around rocks and roots. When we had perhaps reached a foot down, Tammy stood and brushed her hands of dirt.

"I think that is good. Get the book, Elizabeth."

Elizabeth unwrapped it and held it before us. "I don't think I've used anything but a quill before. I am thankful that my father thought even a girl should learn to read and write. There are unscrupulous neighbors who try to forge good names in land grabs."

Tammy scoffed.

"It *happens*! It happened to his sister who could neither read nor write. Her land was signed away by her neighbor, and my father said she died in a ditch!"

Tammy breathed deeply. "We will not die in a ditch, but, Elizabeth, you will have to help Violet and me write our names."

I stood tall. "I can write my name and read a bit, too. Betty taught me."

Tammy appraised me in the moonlight, and it was clear she did not find this news pleasing. "Very well, Elizabeth can help just me, then." She sat on the forest floor and we joined her, though now there was a chill in the air.

Elizabeth opened the book to the first page. "Do I just write my name?"

Tammy shook her head. "No, write what I say; tell me if I go too fast."

Elizabeth nodded. "All right."

"We three named herein do bind ourselves on this night, to form an unbreakable covenant." She paused to let Elizabeth get the words down. "We ask this book to add the names of those who should be punished and let them feel our wrath."

"Oh, my," Elizabeth muttered, "so dark and so many words. I must admit, I am out of practice."

She continued writing, her lips silently forming each of the letters as she went. Finally, she looked up. "Is that it?"

"I think that is enough," Tammy said.

"Should I write my name now?"

Tammy took a small fish knife out of her pocket. "Not with the pencil—with our blood."

CHAPTER FIFTEEN

h, dear." Elizabeth turned to me with wide eyes. "Do you think it *really* must be in blood? You know, maybe it will still work if we just write with pencil."

I sighed, not relishing bloodletting as well. "I'm afraid it seems fitting, but perhaps we use the pencil for our names and then just drip our blood on the page? There are three of us, so just three drops each?"

"That sounds like a *fine* idea to me," Elizabeth jumped in before Tammy could speak. "It would take an *awful* lot of blood to form each letter, and while I will not be missed by my stepfather, Violet should get back sooner rather than later."

"Very well, if it be but a matter of time and not *coward-ice*," Tammy said pointedly.

Elizabeth bristled. "No coward would be sitting under the full moon waiting for a wolf to do her bidding!"

"You are braver than I, Elizabeth, but let us make haste," I implored. "I will admit I am a coward when it comes to the Mistress and Reverend Parris."

Elizabeth nodded and carefully wrote her name. She passed the pencil to Tammy and then wrapped her hand around hers.

"T-A-M-M-Y Y-O-U-N-G-E-R."

When Elizabeth released her hand, Tammy ran a finger along the letters. "This is my name?"

I nodded and thought I could see a touch of annoyance in her eyes as she gave me the pencil. For all her swagger, it was clear she was bothered by being the only one in our trio unable to read and write.

I disregarded her ire and carefully formed the letters in my own name. "Is just *Violet* enough? Though the reverend and the townsfolk always used the name *Indian* when speaking of my family, it was merely what we were, and not a God-given name."

"I think it is enough," Tammy said curtly.

She grabbed the book from my hands and placed it back in her lap. She took the knife out again and, without hesitation, drew a long line across her forearm with its tip.

"Oh, my, oh, dear," Elizabeth whispered, her hand rising to fan her face as three drops of Tammy's blood splashed on the page.

Tammy lifted her skirt and wiped the blood from the knife on her dirty petticoat. "Elizabeth?"

Even in the pale moonlight I could see the color leave Elizabeth's face.

I pushed up my sleeve and held my hand to Tammy. "I'll go next," I said, to give Elizabeth time to bolster her nerves. I took a deep breath and winced as I made a small cut in the crook of my arm and held it over my name. Three drops fell and then I pulled my arm quickly to my chest to stop the bleeding.

"Oh, dear," Elizabeth whispered again, as she held out her hand.

I gave her the knife. "It looks worse than it is, and it doesn't have to be *too* big—just enough for three tiny drops.

She looked up at the moon and then poked the tip of

her thumb. "Ah!" she yelled, and then quickly squeezed three drops onto the page before sticking her thumb in her mouth.

Tammy took the book and blew on the crimson stains. "This is our sacrifice so that our full magic will be born under this full moon." She rewrapped the book in its cloth and stood. "Come; we three will place it in the hole together."

Elizabeth and I stood, and we each laid a hand on the book.

"Show us the first name!" Tammy yelled to the sky, and then we leaned down and placed the book at the bottom of the hole.

My heart began to race. Would some unearthly power really write a name in this book for us to see when we dug it back up?

"Now our bundles on top." Tammy took hers, wrapped in oilcloth, and carefully lowered it in.

"What did you put in it?" Elizabeth whispered.

Tammy grinned. "I told you, it is a surprise."

Elizabeth huffed and then placed her bundle next to

Tammy's. "I bet it is a kitten's whisker; you seem to be quite fond of kittens and they of you."

"You shall see soon enough," she said slyly.

I placed my bundle beside the other two and a thought crossed my mind. "Wait, the coin! I can't return home without more. Do you think it would be possible to magic more?"

"Yes!" Elizabeth squealed. "And I brought an extra egg in case one of ours were to break." She shrugged. "My stepfather says I tend to be clumsy, but perhaps we can wrap the coin with the egg and see what happens?"

"See what happens, indeed," Tammy said. She placed the last bundle with the egg and coin in the hole. She stood tall and inhaled, breathing out slowly. "Throw the dirt in, and as you do, focus your intentions on what we have buried and what we hope to be birthed. Concentrate on those who have wronged us. Concentrate on bringing your familiar to life. Feel the energy in the soil below us and the moon above. Breathe in the air, feel the wind, take it inside you. Bring all this into yourself and watch the magic happen."

Silently, we filled the hole and I struggled in my naming. I was sure Betty's and Abigail's names had passed through Elizabeth's mind, and I could not fault her for that. They had accused her mother along with my own, but Elizabeth's mother had died in prison—she surely held a grudge.

My mind raced.

I once overheard Sheriff Corwin say it was lucky her mother had passed in the jail as it was probably an easier way for a witch to die than by the noose. He followed that statement with a laugh to which others joined in.

I tossed in another handful of dirt.

If we were truly able to make magic tonight, what would become of those named in our book?

I decided to direct my energies on my bundle and the coin.

If I had known it were possible to conjure coins, maybe Papa and I could have magicked some up and paid Mama's bail. And while I admired Elizabeth's wish for a wolf to do her bidding, I knew Mama would approve of my less adventurous choice. Mama loved birds and often spoke of the canaries the plantation owners kept in her homeland. She said they reminded her of home, and she often wished the reverend had brought one or two to Salem, as they would have added some color and song to our gray home.

While a raven was not delicate or colorful like the canaries in her previous home, Mama had told me that her tribe, the Arawak, believed that birds were the connection between the visible and non-visible worlds.

It seemed fitting that a bird might help me bridge those two worlds and reunite me with Mama and Papa.

Tammy and I reached down to grab one of the last handfuls of dirt at the same time and I looked up. Her face was contorted with rage as she flung a fistful into the nearly full hole. Her hair seemed to stand at its roots and dance about her as if it were alive, and I thought she almost had a glow about her.

I glanced at Elizabeth. She was breathing heavily as she concentrated on our task, and I wondered if she felt the same dark energy radiating from Tammy that I did.

"What is next?" I said, dropping the last bit of earth in the hole and stretching my tired muscles.

Tammy patted the earth and carefully redrew the circle

with a stick. When she was done, she looked up and I took a step back. Her eyes were as wild as the feral dogs that roamed the streets last summer.

"We three join hands around this circle. I summon the power from the earth; Violet, the round moon and the twinkling stars; Elizabeth, from the air all around us."

I nodded, though I knew not how to summon anything.

I started to wipe my palms on my dress when Tammy leapt up and snatched my arms, holding them apart. "Leave the earth on your hands; it will connect us."

Her fingers burned against my skin and I half expected to see a mark, but there was none.

She looked up at the moon and then closed her eyes with her arms outstretched. "It is time."

We three stood opposite each other, and Elizabeth and I reached out. The second our hands touched, I gasped. Tremors racked my body as the ground began to tremble under my feet. Leaves rustled as the wind picked up faster and faster, whipping our hair around our faces.

Tammy threw her head back and laughed. "Feel the earth fill us with its energy, feel the moon fill us with its light, feel the wind blow away any doubt that we are strong. Gather it all inside yourself and we will ask—no, we will *demand* the book to write the names of our enemies in blood!"

Elizabeth moaned, tears streaking down her frightened face. "What's happening?"

She tried to rip her hands from mine, but I held them tight.

"Please," she wept, pulling harder. "I don't want to do this anymore. I want to go home!"

"Don't you *dare* let her go, Violet—hold her tight," Tammy growled. "I will have everything I deserve, and *Elizabeth Prince is not going to take that from me!*"

Elizabeth's knees buckled as she tried to wrest her hands from ours. "Let me *go*! Please!"

The wind roared, and tree limbs creaked. Leaves and debris circled us, rising higher and higher into the air. My hands grew moist, and I felt my grasp on Elizabeth start to slide. I looked to the sky for strength and focused on the North Star, faint in the moonlight. "It will be all right, Elizabeth," I called, clutching her tighter.

"You're *hurting* me," she wailed.

The leaves surrounding us suddenly rose high above our heads, and before I could blink, they dropped as if rocks into the center of the circle.

The woods became silent, except for Elizabeth's sobs and the beating of my heart.

"Did we do it?" I asked breathlessly, staring down at the leaves that had settled to fit perfectly into the circle at our feet. "Did it work?"

Tammy dropped our hands and pointed. "Look! It is happening! It is truly happening."

"Oh Lord!" Elizabeth wailed as she scrambled away from the mound pulsing and pushing up from the earth in the center of the circle. "What have we done?" She turned to me and flung herself sobbing into my arms. "Violet! What have we done?"

My breath caught. A sharp, black beak worked its way through the dirt and leaves. The earth writhed, and an ebony-feathered head with eyes as dark as pitch pushed its way out. It blinked and stretched its neck and with a final thrust burst out into the air, showering us with dirt and leaves. A raucous caw pierced the night and my bird, my familiar, flew up into the trees.

"What have we done, Elizabeth?" I turned my chin to the sky and almost felt as if the light of the moon were reaching out to warm me. "We've worked actual magic. *We are witches.*"

CHAPTER SIXTEEN

Elizabeth dropped to my feet, wrapping her arms around my legs. I tugged at her, trying to pull her up. "It's all right. This is what we *wanted*, and we did it! *You* did it. And look!" I gently tilted her chin upward. "There in the branches—that's my bird. It belongs to me."

The raven peered down at us from its perch. Elizabeth grimaced. "I never truly believed. I never truly thought it would work," she said frantically.

The raven fluffed its feathers; dirt drifted down, looking like fabled fairy dust in the moonlight. It cocked its head and trained its eyes on me.

"You are Opias," I declared. "Like the forest spirits from where my parents were born—and stolen from. Now you will help me find where they have been taken to."

"The next should be arriving any time now!" Tammy called. "Be ready."

Elizabeth buried her face in her hands.

Tammy rolled her eyes and stalked over to her. "Get up! A wolf may be coming, and you will need to control it!"

She shook her head and doubled over, rocking as she wept. Tammy grabbed a handful of her blond hair and yanked. "Get up!"

I slapped Tammy's hand away as Elizabeth howled in pain.

"Leave her be!" I bent over to Elizabeth and rubbed her back. "It is all right. These are our familiars, they are a part of us. You need not fear them."

Elizabeth looked up at me, her dirty face streaked with tears. "I do not fear your raven or my wolf. I fear *God*." She pointed to the tree. "That is just a bird," she screamed. "But I have become—no, I have *chosen* to become—the one thing my mother refused to confess! I know my mother was no witch, but she also chose to die rather than lie. She would also die before *this*."

A sob hitched in her throat as she looked to the circle just past us. "I'm making a mockery of her memory."

Tammy knelt by her other side, clutching her shoulder. "You're doing no such thing; you are *avenging* your mother's death. You are honoring her by avenging Violet's mother and father and all the others. I *know* your mother was no witch, but I also know she would want to see you safe."

Elizabeth laughed and shook her head. "*Safe?*"

Tammy loosened her grasp. "Yes, safe. She would want you to have the power to teach the angry men in this town, and those in the next, that they cannot control us—that they can lay a hand on us no more."

"I am torn in two," Elizabeth whimpered. "I thought I wanted this—to be a witch or a folk woman or whatever you call it—but truly, I wished it wouldn't happen. I *hoped* it wouldn't happen and that all this would have been for jest—a small diversion from my miserable life. Tammy, I would have been satisfied to just be your friend and play with the kittens in the barn."

Tammy stood, her face rock-hard. "This is no jest and there is no turning back. We have made a pact—we have signed our names and made a covenant."

Elizabeth looked over to the circle and her lips trembled. "The earth moves again."

My heart raced. Would it be a wolf or kitten next? As the loose dirt rippled, a muffled rattle shook my bones. "Oh, Tammy, no! You didn't?"

Elizabeth's sobs halted as her mouth opened in a silent scream.

She went to bolt, but Tammy grabbed her and then held her tight, turning her to face the circle. "You will watch, and you will see what a powerful woman can conjure."

Tammy smiled gleefully. "My familiar is more powerful than a wolf and it will strike fear in the heart of any man"—she squeezed Elizabeth's arms tighter—"or woman who goes against me."

And there it was: a rattlesnake slithering slowly, inch by inch, out of the circle. Its head rose in the air and then it shook its cream-colored rattle.

Tammy flung her arms back, letting Elizabeth go,

knowing full well she was frozen to the spot. "Watch closely, Elizabeth Prince. Take note."

Tammy slowly approached the snake. Its body was but three feet long, with jagged bands of black lining its sturdy, tan length. I couldn't help wondering whether she was disappointed she hadn't birthed a fully grown familiar, but then my heart stopped as she leaned down inches from its face.

My eyes grew wide. "Tammy, no!"

She looked back at me. "I think I'll call him . . . Bone-Shaker. What do you think of that, *Violet Somebody?*"

My breath caught. "I think on how it is you who seems to read my mind so often, Tammy Younger."

She stroked the snake's head much like one would pet a kitten. She stared into its cold eyes and then turned to me. "I read your face and it shows me what is in your head, Violet. Nothing more."

Tammy picked up the beast, and a shudder racked my body as she draped it across her shoulders and it wrapped itself around her neck. "There's a good Bone-Shaker," she said, nuzzling the top of its head.

Thomas had once dared me to touch a dead garden snake. I was surprised by how cool and smooth its scales were; I'd thought they would be more like that of a slippery frog. I remember how even such a tiny thing, no longer alive and no wider than my little finger, still frightened me.

When I confessed what I'd done to Mama and Papa, they'd talked of the dangerous snakes in their homeland and on the island they lived on before they were bought. They warned me what to watch out for in Salem: the triangle head, the jagged stripes, the death rattle.

A frosty air filled me.

During the witch trials, people often spoke of the familiars sent out to attack their neighbors: cats, dogs, small birds, even rats and pigs.

That Tammy could choose such a wicked creature to be her familiar showed me there was more to her than just her ability to *read* an expression on my face.

It showed me I needed to be careful of my thoughts—careful of everything.

And the way she pulled Elizabeth by the hair—that showed me we were not sisters as I had thought.

CHAPTER SEVENTEEN

h! Oh!" Elizabeth cried. "My bundle—it's opening or hatching or whatever *unholy* thing it is doing underground!" She waved her hands frantically at the circle and then ran to my side. "Violet!"

I took her in my arms, and indeed, the already-disturbed soil was moving again, though ever so slightly. My pulse quickened, imagining how Elizabeth Prince was about to command a wolf, but then I saw not a black nose or a gray snout. There was an orange beak—and brown feathers.

I leaned closer. "Is that . . . a chicken?"

Tammy stared at the circle while rubbing her snake's rattle across her cheek. "Chicken?" She stepped closer as well. "What nonsense is this?"

But there was no doubt: It was a chicken struggling to free itself from the earth, and its clucks were getting louder.

Elizabeth ran to the circle and began to dig with her hands until she'd freed a plain brown hen and then cradled it in her arms.

Tammy spat on the ground. "A *chicken*."

Elizabeth brushed the dirt off the bird, then gently placed it on the ground. "I imagine I may have accidently dropped a few feathers in with the tuft of fur when I wrapped it in my oilcloth. It were but a small tuft, I remember I mentioned that before. And like I said, I thought the fur might be just from a pup, but perhaps the feathers overpowered the tuft." She smiled wanly at us. "I am sure that is how I ended up with a chicken."

Tammy cocked her head. "Are you?"

Elizabeth held her flushed cheeks high. "I am. Regardless, a chicken is a very practical familiar. For instance, if a wolf were sleeping near the house, it would be shot. Really, if a wolf were to be seen *anywhere* in Salem, it would be shot, and I would have to go through this terrifying ceremony once again."

She breathed deep. "I think it is quite fortuitous that I may have put some feathers in the bundle. After all, no one would suspect this particular bird was birthed by magic!"

Elizabeth watched the hen as it clucked and pecked about the circle.

"No one, indeed," Tammy stated flatly.

"And chickens are quite handy at clearing the yard of fleas and ticks. It will do my bidding *and* keep fleas off the dogs!"

A smile broke out on my face. "Elizabeth Prince, this chicken . . . it is the *perfect* familiar for you, and I believe it is laying an egg."

Tammy shook her head in disgust.

"Well!" Elizabeth exclaimed happily. "More eggs make for more magic!"

The hen strained, and a white egg dropped to the ground. Our laughs were cut short when Bone-Shaker rattled its tail and glided down Tammy's arm. In a blink of an eye, it lunged at the chicken, who flapped its wings and scurried away, squawking in alarm.

It was soon clear the hen wasn't the target. Bone-Shaker

unhinged its jaws and I watched in horror as it opened its mouth wide round around the egg and slowly worked it inside its cheeks. Once cleared of the snake's mouth, the egg bulged in its throat and started to work its way down the long body.

Elizabeth carefully walked over to the bird and scooped it up. "Dear Lord, are *any* of us safe from that scaly thing you birthed?"

Tammy laughed. "Too bad you don't have a wolf to protect yourself."

She hung her head. "I really didn't know it was to be a chicken. I swear!"

"Perhaps we should have discussed our familiars' compatibility beforehand," I said wearily.

"Regardless," Tammy said. "Let us see if the three of us were powerful enough to magick some coins."

I knelt and quickly dug my hands into the earth, pulling up tatters of ripped fabric our familiars had been born from. Tiny shell fragments were mixed in the soil, though I felt not a trace of yolk or white.

"Lord," Elizabeth said breathlessly.

I looked up to see her wincing.

"I must say, I am quite happy the birthing happened under the ground. I'm not sure my heart could have endured watching such strange magic before my very eyes."

Tammy stared disbelievingly at her. "It would have been *amazing*; I for one am sorry we could not have borne witness to such an incredible event!"

I dug deeper and felt a solid bundle—the egg clearly intact. I slowly unwrapped it and my heart sunk; only the egg remained. "It's gone—the coin is gone!" I sat back on my heels. "Now I won't have anything for Mistress Parris. She will surely badger Elizabeth's stepfather for going back on his *word* and I will be exposed."

"Crack it open," Tammy said.

"Crack it open? Oh!" Elizabeth nibbled on her fingertips, looking back and forth between us. "*In* the egg? Could that be possible?"

I tapped the egg on my knee, and instead of yolk and white, five coins fell to the ground.

"*There*," Tammy crowed. "There is your payment for delivery of a calf."

Elizabeth whooped. "This is so exciting; my mind is now spinning with possibilities! What other things might we magick on the next full moon? Maybe a new cap even?"

I scooped up the coins, and a wave of relief rushed over me. "Will she think five is a lot for Mr. Osborne to part with?" I turned to Elizabeth. "It is known your family has often found themselves with empty pockets."

Tammy held out her hand. "Give me three; two coins should suffice for feeding a cow some birthing herbs."

I immediately regretted airing my concern, thinking I would need as many coins as possible when I discovered where my parents where. As I reluctantly handed the coins over, I caught Elizabeth frowning as Tammy pocketed them.

I looked up at the moon; it had moved west across the sky and I wondered how long we had been out in the woods. We had one more bundle to dig up and that last one frightened me more than creatures birthed from the earth or coins conjured up. "The book," I whispered.

"Dig it up," Tammy commanded.

I got down on my knees again and leaned over, my fingers curled into the earth, but could not make myself dig, because—what if Mama's name were written in the book?

"Violet? What are you waiting for?" Tammy demanded. "The moon is almost past the clearing."

I summoned the strength I needed to voice the fear in my heart. "What if I gathered all this power inside me, only to find that my mama is the first one to be punished? Or the second? Or the third? How could I live with myself if I was to cause something to happen to her when all I wanted was to be with her again?"

In a blink of an eye, Tammy was by my side, talking rapidly in my ear. "Your mama didn't start this—those girls did. Your mama was the *smart* one! Had she not told those stories, she would be buried in the earth right now and I doubt your Reverend Parris would have paid for even the smallest marker for her grave!"

"She *was* smart," Elizabeth said flatly, staring off into the wood. "If my mother had done the same, she might still be alive. My stepfather had cobbled the coins needed to bail her out, but she would not confess. If only . . ."

She shook her head in disgust. "He spent those coins on drink after we got word of her passing."

I rested my head on my palms. "But my mama didn't *just* confess. She told stories—about people and their familiars—and them signing the Devil's book. *People died.* But maybe it wasn't all just stories. Look what we just did!"

"Did you ever see your mama casting spells?" Tammy asked bluntly. "Did she ever talk of magic?"

Tears streamed down my face. "She read the clouds in the sky—and she could see the future in an egg white. She made guesses about what husbands Betty and Abigail might have . . . They were different each time."

Tammy scoffed. "Foolishness was all that was. Your mother told those judges what they wanted to hear to keep the noose from her neck." She stood and yanked me up and pointed to my raven. "Your mother ever do anything like that?"

Opias stared down at me with a cocked head. He flapped his wings and cawed.

I squeezed my eyes tight. "No. But she talked of spirits from her homeland, not that she ever said she saw one. It was just what her people believed—like the spirits the reverend tells us at service—only from her tribe."

I sighed. "Even the witch-cake she made to see who might be afflicting Betty and Abigail was not her own recipe. Our neighbor Mary Sibley suggested it. But if it were all lies . . . then maybe her name *will* be in the book."

Suddenly Elizabeth shouted. "Oh, hen! Oh, my! Get away from that snake!" She dashed off, chasing after her chicken, who was pecking close to where Bone-Shaker lay coiled, digesting the egg.

"Elizabeth!" Tammy stamped a foot on the ground and it seemed to give off a tremor. She let out an exasperated huff. "Go and dig out the book before I pluck that run-of-the-mill chicken for tomorrow's dinner and share it with the barn cats. And, Violet, I know your mother's name will not be in that book. I can *feel* it!"

I looked up at the moon almost clear of the opening in the trees. "I pray you are right, Tammy."

Elizabeth pushed her arms deep into the dirt. "It's not a run-of-the-mill chicken," she grumbled. "I magicked it!" She pulled up the book, still wrapped in its cloth, and shook it clean.

My heart nearly stopped in my chest as I watched her

slowly loosen the ties. Mama could have confessed to witchery without accusing others. So many people had died. I had weaved magic tonight, dark magic. Would Mama pay the price? Would Mama's name appear on the page when we opened the book?

CHAPTER EIGHTEEN

lizabeth unfolded the fabric and Tammy impatiently grabbed the book from her and placed it in her lap. We gathered around on our knees, peering at its cover.

"Who shall be our first victim?" she sang.

Elizabeth glared at her. "Tammy, I know not how you can be so carefree about this! I hope there is no name at all!"

I held my breath as she opened it and then exhaled with relief.

There was nothing else on the page beside our three names, still spattered with blood.

"Where is the name?" Tammy slapped her hands on the pages. *"We have worked un-Godly magic! Why is there no name?*" Frantically, she flipped blank page after blank page and then turned back to the start. "I don't understand."

A smile broadened my face as relief flooded through me. "Perhaps the moon is telling us that there are none to punish. Perhaps this is a sign the past will stay in the past and we are to move forward."

Tammy shook her head. "No!" she growled. "There should be a name! Martha Wilds assured me we could work this magic with three strong women, and I have hoped with everything I have that at least Mr. *Sewall's* name would appear. That man did so many things to me—so many—at the very least his name *deserves* to be in this book."

To my amazement, I saw that Tammy Younger was crying.

I reached out to her. "Tammy."

She slammed the book to the ground. "And what of your *Betty* and *Abigail* or *Reverend Parris*? How can it be, Violet, that we have conjured familiars—we have magicked coins—but not a single new name appears in this book?"

Her tears softened me, and I leaned against her. "Perhaps our own names are enough?" I whispered. "Perhaps this coven—our friendship—is enough."

Tammy rested her head on my shoulder, and I took the book, opened it on my lap, and sighed. There would be no flight to the stars, and I would have to be content simply being Violet Somebody. I touched the tip of my finger on the V in my name. "Our names will have to be enough," I said definitively.

Suddenly, an icy chill rose from the book into my body, causing bumps to appear on my arms. My teeth chattered uncontrollably. I snatched my hand away as the blood suddenly sunk into the page and the penciled letters disappeared one by one.

"No! No! No!" I swiped my hand repeatedly across the page trying to get them back, hating that I'd set something in motion. "No!"

"What magic now?" Elizabeth whispered frantically, as her name—and then Tammy's—disappeared.

When the last bit of pencil and blood faded, new letters appeared—formed in red, one by one—and Tammy howled with glee.

As soon as I saw the first was a G and not a T, my body shook in relief. "Not Mama."

I held my breath as letter after letter came quickly. I struggled to string each one into a name.

"*George Corwin*," Elizabeth said, before I could work it all out. "Sheriff George Corwin is the first named."

I looked up at them, chilled as if I'd fallen in the stream during the January thaw.

What did it mean to be named in our book?

"What will happen to Sheriff Corwin?" I asked breathlessly.

Tammy grabbed the book from me and drew it to her chest and then held it up to the sky—her wide smile and glistening eyes illuminated in the fading moonlight. "He will get everything he deserves!"

While my skin was clammy and cold, heat—like that from the hearth—was radiating from Tammy.

"And from the tales Elizabeth has told of this man's wretchedness, I for one cannot wait to find out. But now, you best get home, Violet, before your mistress sends someone looking for you—although I would welcome a late-night visit from Thomas Parris."

I looked up at the raven sitting above us in the tree. "Just go? But what next?" It was my turn to speak without pause.

"I know not what to do with myself—I know not what to expect or what to do with Opias. He is my familiar, but he is a stranger to me. How can I sit in the meetinghouse for services tomorrow and see Sheriff Corwin without guilt on my face, a beacon for all to see?"

Tammy raised her skirts. "Become more *familiar* with your familiar." She narrowed her eyes at the coiled snake, and Bone-Shaker rose. "Reach out to your bird; get inside its head." The snake slithered through the underbrush and then wound its way up her leg, coiling around her calf and knee. "As for services—perhaps I should show up as a distraction from Corwin's fate."

Elizabeth stepped back a few paces, gaping. "Services tomorrow? How can you think of services with that creature wrapped around you and not faint—I can barely breathe thinking to be in your place."

Tammy laughed. "*That* is how you control a familiar, and that," she said, dropping the hem of her skirt, "is how you keep it away from prying eyes. Use caution with your raven, Violet. People find them to be an ill omen, and we wouldn't want buckshot headed its way."

Elizabeth cradled her chicken in her arms, staring at

Tammy's skirt. She shuddered. "Luckily for me, I have no need to keep my hen so close to me. It can join the others in the yard. I suppose I will have to find other ways to become familiar with it, such as enjoying its eggs."

"You will do no such thing!" Tammy stated firmly. "We will be using those eggs come the next full moon or perhaps sooner. I know not how often we can conjure spells."

Elizabeth huffed and pouted in Tammy's direction. "Very well. Perhaps I can get some coins next full moon."

Tammy ignored her and turned to me. "Now you, Violet. Command your bird."

I looked up to see my raven's eyes trained on mine.

Could I actually command it?

I held out my arm. "Opias, come!" To my surprise, it suddenly swooped down, landing uneasily on my shoulder. I winced as its talons found their purchase, but felt a bolt of energy—a connection. For just a moment my bones felt hollow and thin like a bird's, and I thought I would fall to the forest floor or even fly up to the sky.

I took a deep breath. Might I really see through this creature's eyes?

As the weight crept back into my body, Tammy nodded approvingly.

"I believe we two have conjured great spies. Martha Wilds told me the longer our familiars are with us, the greater the connection will be. Your Opias will use his wings to travel great distances and my Bone-Shaker will squeeze into cracks and listen to conversations—which will be to our advantage as we use our new power."

"I still think you underestimate my hen," Elizabeth said resentfully. "But it is getting late. My stepfather may have noticed I'm not in bed."

Tammy folded her arms across her chest. "Speaking of your stepfather, I believe it is time we are introduced. I no longer feel being hidden away in barns suits a woman of my great ambition. It is time that I join your household. I can be very persuasive and believe I can convince the man that he needs a girl to help you run the house and farm—or perhaps I am a cousin your mother neglected to mention."

"B-but, Tammy . . . ," Elizabeth began. "We really do not have coin to pay you for work we could do ourselves—and it is risky to make up family ties that could be exposed."

Tammy winked. "'Tis only for room and board I will ask of my dear, sweet stepuncle. But it is time I became a proper resident of Salem. How else am I to begin my official courtship with Thomas Parris?"

I scoffed. "Tammy, you are but fourteen. You are years off from being of courtship age."

She looked down her nose at me. "His kisses prove otherwise, but I am of the age where I need to think of my future. I need to become a respectable member of Salem, and with this book doing my bidding, I shall. I will pick whom I wish to marry—be it Thomas Parris or some other upstanding young man I discover when I am welcomed at service as the new girl at the Osborne-Prince farm."

"My house does not have the reputation you seek, Tammy," Elizabeth said.

"Then I will pick and choose which other houses to work at as I make my way to the top of Salem's society."

"This isn't Gloucester and it's *our* bidding," Elizabeth snipped. "And I'm not sure why you think yourself to be in charge."

Tammy looked down her nose at Elizabeth and folded

her arms. "Who said I am in charge?"

Elizabeth folded her arms across her chest, mirroring Tammy. "You said the book would do *your* bidding, but we are a coven of three. The book does *our* bidding. And you are not in Gloucester. People are not so free about things here. People may not hang witches anymore, but they do not approve of them either."

Tammy laughed and waved a hand in the air. "I am bringing Gloucester's new way of thinking to Salem, and yes, of course the book does *our* bidding. You can certainly write the name of your future husband on these pages; fill every page with your silly desires, for all I care. Unlike Violet's mother, *our* future casting will come true and we shall have anything we long for, and what I desire—for now," she said coyly, "is Thomas Parris."

I bit my tongue. The Parris family would never embrace Tammy Younger as a suitable match for their Thomas. And though the reverend was not well liked in town, Thomas was. He lacked his father's arrogance, and though some would malign him for simply being a Parris—unlike his parents—Thomas had a warmth to him.

At least I think he did. Since I returned from Gloucester, Thomas Parris had kept to himself with hardly a look my way. Seeing him with Tammy was the happiest he'd looked in months. Maybe there was something to Tammy's prediction that she would be his wife, but if she put her wishes in the book, would Thomas be magically bound to her forever?

Did we have the right to take that choice away from him?

I thought Thomas might disappoint Tammy under the watchful eyes of Salem. Certainly, at services he could not fawn over her as she was accustomed in the shade of the oaks and maples.

Of course, it would be years before Thomas would be ready to take a wife. The immediate question was, would Tammy find a way to be at services tomorrow, and if so, how would Thomas react to seeing her out of the shadow of the woods and under the glaring light of the Salem congregation?

Tammy Younger may have thought that she brought her progressive ideas to Salem, but she had not yet sat through a day-long service led by the Reverend Parris. We may have wrought magic tonight, but we still were but three young girls under the thumb of all above us.

CHAPTER NINETEEN

lizabeth cleared her throat, and her eyes pleaded for me to give a word on the matter at hand, but I had none I was willing to voice in front of Tammy.

She exhaled with obvious disgust. "If you wish to speak to my stepfather, Tammy, I will not stop you. He has been a cold man long before my mother passed, but I suppose if anyone could persuade him to take on another mouth we can ill afford, it would no doubt be *you.*"

"Well, he has been feeding me—he just doesn't know it—but I rather like the idea that I am a long-lost cousin. With your mother dead, you can vouch for me and come evening you and I will share a bed and I can be done with the vermin in the barn." Tammy grinned, though it was clear to me that Elizabeth thought the prospect of moving Tammy from the barn into the household was nothing to smile about.

The snake rattled softly and it sent shivers down my spine.

Or perhaps Elizabeth wanted to keep some distance between them. I knew I did. I had just signed my name in a book and bonded myself to these girls—one of whom had shown herself to be reckless—no, *dangerous*—with her choices.

Looking up at Opias, who was now perched on a branch, I knew I was lying to myself.

I had known Tammy Younger was dangerous the moment I met her, yet I willingly went along with everything.

She spoke of revenge from the start, and even though that was not my motivation for joining the coven, I had helped set this new storm into motion, and I feared I would be helpless to stop it.

I was not surprised to see Sheriff Corwin's name appear on the page, though. He had ruled the village of Salem through intimidation afforded by his high standing and wealth and became more and more ruthless as accusations had mounted.

John and Elizabeth Proctor had barely been accused of witchery and taken to jail when he swooped in with his men and looted their home, selling their livestock and belongings. The Proctors were not the only ones to have their things taken before a trial had even begun.

But looting was tame compared to Sheriff Corwin's treatment of the accused. People had their arms and legs tied together behind their backs for days until they confessed—or not—but it was his treatment of Giles Corey that showed how truly vicious Corwin was.

Mr. Corey was a cantankerous man, bent and withered by seven decades on earth, and he had even joined my Betty, Abigail, and the other girls in accusing his own wife of bewitching their animals. When Ann Putnam Jr. accused Mr. Corey of sending his spectral self to her, no one was more surprised than Mr. Corey himself.

When the judge asked him how he should be tried, Giles Corey refused to respond, preventing his trial from beginning.

Sheriff Corwin thought he could get an answer they

needed, though. Over a period of days, the sheriff had his men pile rocks on Mr. Corey's naked body, hoping to force an answer out of him.

People still whisper how Giles's swollen and parched tongue lolled out of his mouth on the second evening and the sheriff simply pushed it back in with the tip of his cane, still hoping the man would speak.

Finally, on the third day, Mr. Corey—eyes bulging, lungs struggling to take in air under the large pile of stones— took his last breath, remaining mute to the end.

If there was anyone more disliked than Reverend Parris, it was surely Sheriff Corwin, but he had a new wife and a young son, Bartholomew, who had taken his first steps but a year and a half ago. I could not deny he was a terrible man, but did he deserve our unearthly revenge?

I supposed Giles Corey might think so.

And Elizabeth's mother.

I looked at the night sky through the clearing again. More stars showed themselves now that the moon had traveled farther across the sky—the North Star gleamed brighter than them all. I scowled. Perhaps the North Star would have no name for me but *witch*. Tonight, I took little comfort knowing it was also shining down on Mama and Papa, wherever they were. Mama was probably braiding her hair for bed and perhaps Papa was rubbing ointment on his arthritic hands so they would be ready to work the next day. Tonight, I feared they'd be ashamed of me if they knew what I had done.

I had signed my name and shed my blood because I wanted to be with my family again. Unlike Elizabeth, I had prayed we would be granted powers tonight, but now that I had seen creatures conjured from bits of scale and feather and a name written by magic, I feared that Tammy's thirst for revenge might do real harm. And whatever happened, I would have to carry part of the blame on my own shoulders.

Did Mama feel that same kind of weight?

I felt a heaviness in my chest as if all the trees were falling on top of me. "I need to go home," I said, as tears sprung to my eyes.

Tammy grabbed my shoulders, and I braced myself as she faced me. My chest puffed when I felt no surge of power from her fingers as she squeezed. "He will get what he deserves, Violet, and the next named as well. We live in a world of hard hearts and we need to fight against those who beat us down. Accept what the universe has given us with no remorse; embrace it."

I looked into her eyes. "I have been given a *raven*. I do not have what I most desire."

"Patience is a virtue, Violet. You cannot find your family without sacrifice. The book will reveal all in its time."

More tears flowed as she echoed my father's nightly advice. Did Tammy somehow know my father said those words to me every night while we talked about saving enough money to bring Mama home? Could she really read my mind and somehow steal my memories and use them against me? I pulled myself away wondering if there was something I could write in that book to keep Tammy Younger out of my head.

"Just what am I sacrificing?" I asked. "I wish I knew. And I wish I were as confident as you that my mother's name will not appear in the book. I will see you at service tomorrow," I said to Elizabeth, "and perhaps you as well, Tammy."

Tammy narrowed her eyes. "You can count on it, Violet."

"Wait," Elizabeth said, rushing toward us. She stopped, her shoulders rounded and her head low. "Before we go, I need to know: Are either of you as scared as I for what tomorrow might bring?"

Tammy shook her head. "Not in the least!" she said unequivocally, hugging the book to her breast. "We just need to go through one page at a time, and then I know the world will be ours to rule."

I stared at the book. "I wonder if we shall feel satisfied when we rule the world with the taste of revenge on our lips?"

Tammy scoffed. "Harden your heart, Violet *Indian*. You must be tougher and stronger than the people who stole your parents from their tribe, sold them, and then sold them again without a thought that *Indians* might mourn being torn from their land or mourn being torn from their only child without even a goodbye."

She gave me a self-satisfied smile as I fought back new tears. "You do know that's why you were sent to Gloucester, don't you? So your reverend could arrange for your parents' sale without a little thing like *you* getting in the way. Just imagine the scene you would have made watching your father being taken away in a cart to parts unknown. What a scandal that would have been! What would the neighbors have said?"

She cocked her head. "Actually, I think the neighbors would have paid little mind; after all, you are just an Indian. Betty and Abigail certainly had no qualms accusing *Mama Tituba* of witchcraft."

My lips trembled as a cry caught in my throat. "I thought we were sisters," I whispered.

"Yes, you thought that because you sit with these people at services, eat with them at a shared table, but you are not one of them. *Harden your heart*, and accept what the book shows us. This is the only path to your parents. You told me you had a darkness in you—*use* it!"

Before I could even think how to use "darkness," she turned to Elizabeth.

"And you, you're frightened? Think of how frightened your mother felt sitting in a cold, damp cell for nine weeks, praying to a God who did not answer her. And does the town mourn the passing of a woman who took up with her hired hand? I have heard the tongues wagging of your mother, living under the same roof with Alexander Osborne, an indentured servant she hired and then wed. If your stepfather loses the farm, you will be in the same boat I was. Working in some home at the mercy of the mistress and master. Harden your heart, Elizabeth Prince, find your backbone, and relish our power."

"I suppose you'll tell us you heard all this in *Gloucester!*" Elizabeth spat.

"No," Tammy said calmly, "I heard it here in Salem. I listen from the shadows. The trials are over, people are dead, but the gossip lives on."

CHAPTER TWENTY

lizabeth stalked away and snatched up her chicken, who let out a loud squawk. "My mother did what she had to do to keep the farm, and then she did what she had to do to save her soul. I only wish I had a small part of her courage, but I will tell you that I am indeed frightened and no matter what gossip or horror stories you tell, I will not harden my heart just because you say I should!"

Tammy laughed. "Did you hear Sheriff Corwin interrogate your mother? How about you, Violet?" she asked, turning back to me. "Was he a *kind* man trying to get to the bottom of a bewitching to save the poor, afflicted girls, or was he a merciless land-grabber wishing to top off his already-bursting coffers? Shall I go on? Do you need more reasons to praise the heavens that George Corwin's name is in our book?"

I was struck dumb by her speech. Tammy had the power to twist your insides and scramble your head until you didn't know what was up or down. At that moment, all I wished was to put as much space as possible between the two of us.

I peered around into the trees looking for a path. With the moon farther away, the darkness had filled the wood with shadows. "Opias, lead me home."

"Wait, Violet!" Tammy called. "We need to make a plan. We need to make sure I will be accepted in the village. I need to know who I should talk to and how."

I stared at her coldly. "If you go to services tomorrow, there will be none to talk to. You will simply sit in the balcony with the other lowborn and listen to Reverend Parris. And whether the people of Salem accept you is your concern, not mine, but you seem quite capable of convincing people to do your bidding. And really, what advice could an *Indian* such as I have to offer you?"

She put her hands on her hips. "*Violet*," she said, sounding wounded.

"I need to get home, Tammy, or I will get a whipping. If you are to be at services tomorrow, you have work to do. I suggest you start washing and mending your dress. Opias!"

I held out my arm, and Opias swooped down with barely a flap of his wings and landed lightly on my shoulder. His talons seemed to rest easier this time, perhaps getting used to this perch, perhaps getting used to me. He cocked his head and trilled, but I still knew not what to do. He looked at me, waiting, and I closed my eyes and pictured my home, no, the Parrises' home, in my head. "Show me the way through the woods."

"Violet!"

I ignored Tammy as Opias's stiff feathers stroked my cheek. He lifted into the air and landed in a tree to my left, and I quickly, but carefully, made my way toward him, following him from tree to tree. Before long, the stream could be heard, and the familiar path I took for gathering kindling was underfoot. We made our way to the clearing, and I froze as I looked out at the Parris house in the distance.

What would await me when I walked through the door? Like Elizabeth, I feared what tomorrow would bring.

I reached into my apron pocket and fingered the coins Tammy gave me. Mistress Parris would no doubt be pleased, but my long black hair tumbling down my back would be a problem—an affront to God.

Would the coins be enough to make Mistress Parris forgive my missing cap?

I bowed my head. The cap was the least of my concerns.

What would become of Sheriff Corwin?

Opias cawed. The house was in view, and I wondered—no, hoped—the raven might do what Tammy had spoken of.

Could he spy for me?

I closed my eyes again and pictured the streets of Salem leading from the Parris house to Sheriff Corwin's. "Show me. Look in the windows," I whispered.

My eyes shot open as Opias cawed loudly in my ear, and I watched his dark form fly into the night. I carefully made my way to the house and opened the door. Mistress Parris was sitting in a chair knitting. She slowly put the needles down and glared at me with such disgust, my blood ran cold.

"Where is your cap, Violet?"

"The cow snatched it from my head, but I have two

coins!" I quickly fished the coins out of my pocket and dropped them on the table.

Relief spread through me as her eyes left mine and looked to the coins. "It is fortunate for you that it was not your last cap."

I bowed my head. "Betty and Abigail, are they well?"

"Well enough. They are sleeping. I have done your chores, so get to bed. We must rise early for services."

I nodded and made my way to my room and quickly changed into my nightshirt. I slipped between the cool sheets and pulled the rough blanket to my chin.

Lying there, I tried to see if I felt different now that I was a witch, but in the dark, I felt every bit the same Violet I had been this morning. I still cowered under Mistress's glare, and tomorrow I would set the table as always.

A nervous tickle fluttered in my stomach. This morning I had not a bird that had burst out of the earth or a book of names or girls with whom I'd made magic.

I clasped my hands to my chest.

I had made magic tonight, *real* magic, and I realized it had nothing to do with the Devil and everything to do with longing and anger and heartbreak. Just three broken girls joined together, summoning the power of the earth, the moon, and the air we breathed.

Three girls at odds on how to wield our power.

I wanted to deny that Betty and Abigail were truly bewitched, but how could I now? Perhaps they had just thought it was Mama and Sarah Osborne and Sarah Good.

Perhaps Mama had just thought things, too.

I shook my head. Mama slept in this room every night. She was not out flying on poles and meeting with folk in the woods.

Or was she? How could I be sure of anything anymore?

A caw echoed loudly in my head, and I bolted up in my bed. My head turned from side to side, thinking Opias was in the room with me, for that was how it felt. My heart pounded as everything slipped away, and I found myself peering through a hazy window into a room lit with candles.

I felt talons clutch the window frame as if they were my own toes. I felt the cool night air ruffle feathers as though it were my own hair.

A woman's screams ripped through me. Claws gripped the windowsill and I felt the urge to fly away. My own toes clenched.

I gasped. I was seeing through Opias's eyes.

I was Opias.

I blinked, trying to erase the picture, but I could not separate myself from him.

Though all I wanted was to be me, safe in my bedroom, I needed to see what was happening.

Stay! I commanded. *Watch!*

A baby wailed from another room.

"George! George!" a woman cried frantically.

Opias cawed loudly, and I saw it was Mistress Corwin looking up from where she was kneeling to the window. I felt her eyes on me, but it was Opias she was seeing—and through his eyes, I saw a body in front of her splayed out on the floor. The sheriff.

Her hand flew to her mouth as she screamed again and her son's wails grew louder.

I could feel fear coursing through Opias, coursing through me. Then he flapped his wings to fly off into the night.

I was back in my own room, blood pounding in my head, trying to block the images of Mistress Corwin hovering over her husband on the floor, his eyes open, but no longer seeing.

My heart pounded, and I struggled to take a breath.

Was Sheriff Corwin truly dead? And if that were true, there was no other explanation except that I—no, *we*— were responsible for his death.

CHAPTER TWENTY-ONE

I woke the next morning to a loud knocking at the front door. I rushed into my day clothes, as heavy feet pounded down the stairs. I tied my hair back and put on my old cap, shocked I had been able to find any sleep at all.

I had all but held my breath the whole night, hoping to find I had simply dreamed the vision at the Corwins' and the sheriff was still alive, but somehow sleep had found me.

Opening my bedroom door just a sliver, I heard Mr. Putnum and the reverend in heated conversation.

"When did it happen?"

"Not long past midnight. Lydia Corwin said he awoke with pains in his chest. He got out of bed and couldn't stop pacing and then his heart just gave out."

Reverend Parris bowed his head as I exhaled.

It was no dream; it had really happened. I leaned against the wall as my legs seemed ready to buckle.

"I hesitate to tell you this"—Mr. Putnam lowered his voice—"but right after he fell, she saw a large black bird—a crow—peering through the window. She said there was no mistaking, it was looking right at her. You know what this means, don't you?"

The reverend's face darkened, and he drew a fist to his chin. "It is an ill omen. Corwin was but thirty years old and appeared to be in good health. Was the bird sent by someone with malice on their mind or by the very Devil himself?"

My legs shook, and I felt as if my own heart might give out. It was easy to hope a vision seen after a strange night in the woods could be fantasy or delirium, but the sheriff was indeed dead—because of me, because I stole that book.

And Mistress Corwin had seen Opias.

I wanted to blame it all on Tammy, but without the stolen book, there would have been no name and I had spilled my blood on the page the same as she. I felt as if I could burst into a million pieces. I deserved it—I had killed someone—a young boy was fatherless.

Reverend Parris pounded his fist into his other hand. "Since the governor warned us to keep all 'frivolous' suspicions of witchcraft at bay, those who sign the Devil's book may have become emboldened. Best to keep that piece of it to yourself as to not alarm the village, but cast a sharp eye for other signs that witchcraft may be infecting us again."

Mr. Putnam pursed his lips and cocked his head. "Again . . . or for the first time?"

The reverend stiffened. "*Again*," he said pointedly.

The two eyed each other and it seemed clear to me that Mr. Putnam was not in agreement with the reverend. "There is one more thing, Parris. Phillip English has put a *lien* on Corwin's corpse."

"What madness is this?"

"It is well-known Corwin was quick to seize the property of the accused before they had even been tried. English lost a great deal before he was pardoned, so he's put a lien on the corpse, demanding reimbursement from Corwin's estate. There are whispers others may follow suit. As you can imagine, Lydia is worried that even if she is cleared to bury his body, his resting place may be vandalized by any number of others who felt . . . *abused* by the sheriff."

"I will talk sense into English before services today. Corwin—and anyone—should have a proper burial, no matter how . . . *disliked* they were. Leave me, I must amend my sermon to reflect his passing and to keep others from following English's lead. I fear dark times may be upon us again."

"*Again.* You keep saying the word, but it doesn't erase the past—erase what we did or allowed to be done or said. These are dark times of our own making. Or perhaps the Devil has really come to Salem to make us pay for our sins?"

The reverend looked up at the ceiling, and I thought he was thinking of Betty and Abigail sleeping above him. "You talk in riddles, Putnam."

Mr. Putnam folded his hands across his chest. "Perhaps you and I have a different understanding of what went on, or perhaps you are in denial."

The reverend shook his head. "I know only God's word."

"Well, you had best use God's words to convince whomever sent that bird to shun Satan's grasp, Reverend. There are many who still bear the scars of Corwin's interrogations. Lydia is right to fear the desecration of her husband's grave—or even that of his body." He hung his head. "These are things I fear myself."

The reverend drew back. "Oh?"

"Parris," Mr. Putnam began, in a hushed voice, "God forgives those who repent. I am not wrong in thinking that to be true?"

"Do you have *things* you wish to repent?"

"Don't you?"

The reverend stood tall. "No man is without sin."

Mr. Putnam nodded. "I have perhaps behaved in an un-Godly manner in the past. Hearing that Lydia saw that bird, well, it has given me a terrible pause. I am not . . . proud of some things I have done—claims that were made under false pretense. I fear a dark bird may come to my own window. I fear for myself and my wife and my little Ann." Mr. Putnam looked the reverend in the eye. "You should fear the bird, too."

The reverend turned away from him. "I have no reason

to fear some black bird coming to my window—I have always behaved in a Godly manner. My conscious is clear."

"Have you? There are some that would dispute that, and what of your girls?"

The reverend stiffened. "And what of your little Ann?" he shot back coldly. "And her mother? And you? I'll have you remember no accusations ever came from *my* lips."

Mr. Putnam nodded. "No. Not from your lips—just your girls and that servant of yours. Necks snapped because of them. I am not guilt-free, but I am at least owning up to what I did, and I hope God is listening and can forgive me."

The two stood glaring at each other until Mr. Putnam looked away. "I will keep quiet about the bird, Parris, and hope that if Lydia Corwin spoke the truth, God has indeed forgiven me and will shield me from a fate such as Corwin's. The Lord knows my sins pale compared to his, but still I fear. I hope you and your girls are shielded as well, for we all know that the madness started in this very house."

He looked around the room, and I thought he might be searching for spirits, but it was clear from his expression he found this to be just an everyday room in an uncommon house.

This home might not have housed evil spirits, but it carried a heavy weight. I could feel the air pressing on me, and I thought Mr. Putnam and the reverend did as well.

Mr. Putnam brought his hand to his mouth as his eyes darted around the room. "God protect you, Reverend Parris. God protect us both."

He placed his hat on his head and left.

The reverend walked to the bookshelf and took a Bible into his hands and brought it to his chest. "God, protect Betty and Abigail, let them be free of Satan's grasp, and let them repent their lies."

Reverend Parris sat at his desk and began to write in his sermon book as I carefully closed my door, lifting the latch so the bottom of the door would not scrape against the floor.

I looked out the window, taking in the fog that kept the rising sun at bay.

Lies.

Did *lies* send my mother to prison? Did *lies* cause Mama to tell stories to protect herself or to inflict harm?

Or both?

Would she have told such tales if she knew what would

happen—if she knew how many would die?

The reverend seemed truly concerned that dark magic had crept back into Salem—he seemed to believe it. Yet I felt—no, I knew—his prayer to God showed me he was all too aware that Betty and Abigail were liars and he was worried for their souls.

How many had people died before he discovered the truth about their tales?

I could not answer my own question, but it was clear—both lies and magic had the power to kill.

I sat at the end of my bed and folded my hands in my lap.

"Mama lied," I whispered to the fog.

My body rocked back and forth.

I had known that for a while now, but I had yet to say it out loud until just then.

My heart ached.

Mama and Betty and Abigail and Ann Putnam and Mercy Lewis and all the others had lied, knowing people would die.

Why did they do it?

My chin sunk to my chest.

Why had I signed my name in a book? Had I become so accustomed to death that I thought it would not affect me? That I would not be overcome with guilt and remorse that a small boy was now fatherless?

I had prayed for magic, but I had not prayed for death.

Was it too late to prevent another person's name from appearing in blood in our book or would it come at the next full moon?

What were the rules, if there even were some?

Would Mama's name be written in my own blood?

I shuddered.

Mama may not have known the deaths her stories would bring, but I now knew what the book I stole was capable of. I had not known exactly what form *revenge* might take, but in the back of my mind I surely knew death was a possibility.

The reverend was right, though—dark times had indeed come back to Salem.

I buried my face in my hands. Mama had recanted her confession—she said Reverend Parris had beaten it out of her—but how could she have known that her story would be used to make others suffer, to steal their land and possessions?

Mr. Putnam was frightened; I saw his haunted eyes. He had all but admitted his family's many accusations of witchery were lies, and the reverend had just asked God to save Betty and Abigail because . . . he feared they both might share the same fate as Sheriff Corwin's.

I think they both knew that things were different this time.

Betty and Abigail started a lie about magic—but now, the magic was real.

I needed to talk to Elizabeth; we had to figure out how to stop this. I needed to talk to her without Tammy around, twisting words and making it seem like this was all fine or something I even wanted. All I wanted were Mama and Papa, not this.

"Violet!" Mistress Parris barked as she opened my door, causing me to jump. "Why is the hearth cold and the table not yet set?"

"Sheriff Corwin is dead," I said hurriedly, rising to face her.

She sniffed, and our eyes met. It was clear she had no

tears for the sheriff, perhaps no tears for anyone. "I have heard, and I have prayed for Mistress Corwin, but still the sun rises, and we must carry on. Make haste, Violet, it will be a busy day."

She turned and left the room.

I felt her coldness wash over me and I knew just then that I could not endure any more cold, any more darkness. It was at that moment I rejected Tammy's command.

I rejected Mistress Parris.

I would not harden my heart—I could not.

I did not wish to be like Mistress Parris or Tammy or any of those who lived without light.

I could not walk in my mother's shoes. She had faced more horrors in her life than I could even imagine, but I would have no more blood spilled upon my family with no name.

I would not let these people steal the light I once had, the lightness Mama had given me or the quiet peacefulness Papa had shared every evening.

My mind reeled. I had to get my hands on the book, but I had to tread carefully.

Tammy was determined—but so was I.

CHAPTER TWENTY-TWO

We made our way to the meetinghouse with a gloom still hanging in the air. Fog swirled in eddies that the late-spring sun seemed unable to burn off, and I hoped it wasn't an omen signaling that the day would never find its light—a light I was hoping to reclaim.

Thomas walked swiftly in front, while Betty and Abigail took labored steps behind Reverend and Mistress Parris. By now, word had spread of the sheriff's death and though he was disliked, I thought no one would show anything but sadness in public. Even Mistress Parris dabbed her dry eyes every minute or so as she nodded to people we passed.

I entered the meetinghouse and the air hummed with

whispers. Lydia Corwin sat clutching her son to her chest as women of stature huddled around her where the men usually sat. I shouldn't have been surprised, but I was shocked that some who were standing to the side or up in the gallery could barely conceal their glee to see Mistress Corwin's sobbing.

Tammy surely would be pleased to see such open contempt, but it saddened me that such callousness was present in a house of worship. Arms were folded across chests, and many faces showed not even the pretense of mourning. The ugliness on display made me more determined to get Elizabeth alone and find out where she and Tammy had hidden our book. I could not stand another day knowing we had caused this tragedy.

I bowed my head. Was it even possible to stop another?

Could Tammy look on Mistress Corwin and not feel for her and her child? I hoped she could; I hoped she would agree to destroy the book.

I looked up to the balcony—usually the girls would have their heads bent together to gossip—but today, all eyes were trained down on Mistress Corwin.

The Widow Corwin.

We had caused this—Tammy, Elizabeth, and me.

I couldn't take back what we did, but I had to stop it from continuing.

But would ripping out the pages with our blood prevent another tragedy? Would it be enough to break our pact?

I bowed my head and made my way upstairs, and no one paid me, Violet Indian, any mind. I took my usual seat and marveled at the quiet, growing undercurrent of whispers beginning to overwhelm my senses.

He had it coming.

It's a wonder it didn't happen sooner.

It was God's doing—it's retribution for what he did.

The Devil finally came to claim one of his own.

Mistress Corwin saw a crow at her window when it happened.

That is the Devil's work for sure.

People had heard about Opias at the Corwins' window.

I heard fear in their voices. They were afraid my Opias might visit them, not knowing it was the book that was the harbinger of death and not my bird.

From my seat, the rush of hushed voices engulfed me. Some voices snickered—and then all was quiet.

"Who is that?" Mercy Lewis asked, pointing to the main level.

I looked down and saw that Mr. Osborne, Elizabeth, and Tammy had entered the meetinghouse with Elizabeth's brothers.

Tammy held her head high and she was wearing what was obviously one of Elizabeth's dresses, though she filled it out much better. Even from the balcony I could see she had reddened her lips. I shook my head—this would not go over well. Mr. Osborne introduced Tammy as his late wife's niece to the people closest to the door and she beamed as heads turned her way.

Mr. Danvers took Mr. Osborne aside and there was a hushed exchange. Mr. Osborne then turned to Mistress Corwin and bowed his head. "Sorry for your loss," he said.

I watched Elizabeth pale at his side as she took in the news.

Ashen, she turned to Tammy, who could barely contain glee. Elizabeth looked up to the balcony. I nodded as her horror-filled eyes met mine. She pulled Tammy to the steps and dragged her up as she rushed to my side.

"When did it happen?" she whispered frantically, her eyes darting around at the other girls.

"Last night."

"We did it, we actually did it!" Tammy exclaimed.

"Hush!" Elizabeth cried. She leaned in toward us. "We must not let on that we had anything to do with this," she whispered.

"Where is the book?" I asked. "We have to destroy it before another is named."

Elizabeth nodded as Tammy looked incredulously at us. "Are you mad? This is what we want; this is only the beginning."

"Where is the book?" I asked again.

Tammy tilted her chin up. "Someplace safe."

Deep down, I had known what kind of person Tammy was. I had just underestimated her resolve—her true ruthlessness.

"Elizabeth?" I implored.

"I know not where it is. I wanted nothing to do with it;

I went to my room to await Tammy's *arrival* at our door in the early morning."

"I must say your stepfather was most gracious taking in a long-lost niece," Tammy said with a smirk. "Thank you for vouching for me, Elizabeth."

I put my hand on Tammy's arm. "Is it in the barn, or did you leave it in the woods?"

"It is someplace safe. I will check for another name, but I obviously cannot trust you two with it. Your change of hearts is most unfortunate, but I will not be swayed from seeing this through to the end."

"Tammy, this is serious," I said. "That boy down there is without a father."

She sniffed. "Mistress Corwin will no doubt marry again—I'm sure her wealth will draw any numbers of suitors."

Elizabeth stared at her. "How can you be so heartless?"

"I prefer the word *cold*," she said matter-of-factly. "I just hope we don't have to wait until the next full moon to see another name, but I will keep you both apprised. Oh, there is Thomas. Excuse me, please, ladies."

I clutched her wrist as she started to stand and pulled her back to the seat. "It is not proper to go to Thomas," I warned, through gritted teeth.

She pulled her arm from my grasp and rose, looking down her nose at me. "What makes you think I care about truly being proper?" She laughed. "I thought you knew me better than that, Violet."

"Tammy," I whispered, "you have to be careful. You are new here and all eyes will be on you. All eyes will be judging you—watching your every move. If you want to be accepted in Salem, you must heed our warnings."

She shook her head and rolled her eyes as if I were a child still learning how the world works. "I make my own rules, Violet, and with our book, I will be the next sheriff of Salem if I so choose!"

She promenaded away, casting a disdainful glance at the other girls, and made her way down the stairs.

I stared after her with an open mouth.

Elizabeth buried her head in her hands.

"We have to find the book," I implored, turning to Elizabeth.

"I am shaken to the core," she said. "And to think my stepfather has welcomed her into our home! Of course, I have no one to blame but myself, but I now have to share my bed with her! How can I sleep, knowing I am lying next to a monster? And she is a monster. Look at her. I wish she had never made her way to Salem. I wish everything could just go back to the way it was."

Below, Tammy sauntered over to Thomas, who looked at her with surprise.

Mercy Lewis sat down suddenly next to Elizabeth. "Who is that girl?" she asked, her eyes filled with jealousy. "Did I hear correctly that she is your cousin?"

Elizabeth nodded. "Yes, Tammy—Tammy Younger. We had not spent much time with her part of the family before my mother passed, but she will be staying with us . . . indefinitely it seems."

"Pity for you." Mercy narrowed her eyes. "Has she rouged her lips?"

"It is only strawberries," Elizabeth said, her cheeks flushing. "She was eating strawberries. I am sure it was not intentional that she stained her lips, but I did caution her."

Mercy curled her lip. "Well, you should have cautioned her more strongly. I suggest you let your cousin know that is not how we do things around here, especially on the Sabbath. A girl like her could very well end up in the stocks. And look at poor Thomas. It is obvious he is quite uncomfortable to be around a girl who would rouge her lips."

She stood and looked down at me. "I would also caution you to mind the company you keep, lest you be judged as well, Elizabeth Prince."

CHAPTER TWENTY-THREE

ercy left to join the older girls, I bowed my head as a cold, clammy feeling filled me up.

Was she referring to Tammy or me?

Was I someone Elizabeth should be ashamed to be with?

Elizabeth reached out and put a hand on my knee. "Don't let her words touch you, Violet. Mercy Lewis does not know the things we know. Though she—"

"She what?

Elizabeth looked away. "Mercy has also lost both her parents," she said softly.

I nodded. Mercy Lewis's parents were slain by Wabanaki Indians. I wished I could tell her how peaceful Mama and Papa's people were—that they were stolen from their homeland—but that is not a tale that would console Mercy or perhaps change her thoughts about me.

I looked down to see Tammy try to sidle up to Thomas.

Thomas did indeed look uncomfortable. Tammy smiled at him in a knowing way, and he blushed and shook his head. I could not hear what he told her, but he quickly turned away and took his seat with the other young men, and I could see her face cloud over.

If only Thomas knew how much of a viper Tammy was and that his very life could be in danger by crossing her.

Suddenly all whispers ceased; Mr. English had entered the meetinghouse with the reverend right behind. "*English*, see reason," the reverend implored.

"I will have restitution, Parris," he declared, looking past the reverend at Mistress Corwin. "And I encourage anyone else who was robbed by the late sheriff," he proclaimed loudly, "to make a claim on his estate as well!"

"This is not the time or place for such talk, English!" Reverend Parris exclaimed.

Mistress Corwin's face crumpled, and she hurriedly made her way to the benches toward the back, surrounded by a protective group of women.

Mr. English eyed her, and it was clear he was staying resolute with his promise to keep a lien on the sheriff's body.

The reverend motioned for everyone to take their seats. Elizabeth bowed her head and ignored Tammy as she rejoined us. But I saw Tammy boldly stare at all the girls eyeing her. She sat down next to Elizabeth and folded her arms across her chest.

"You would think these girls had never seen a strong girl from Gloucester." She sniffed. "It is obvious they sense Thomas is sweet for me."

"I told you it was not proper to go to Thomas," I whispered as the reverend started on his opening remarks. "It was unseemly."

"I care not," Tammy declared, "but I will meet with Thomas later, when we can be alone without the prying eyes of these busybody girls."

I looked down at Thomas. If he could meet Tammy in the woods, then Elizabeth and I could search for the book. I saw him look up to the gallery, and Tammy beamed at him. He quickly turned away, and I wondered if he was having second thoughts about kissing a girl like Tammy. Seeing her boldly approach him with rouged lips, I wondered if he would agree to meet with Tammy or perhaps set his sights on a more proper girl like Mercy Lewis, who knew how to obey the rules.

I bit my lip. He just *had* to meet her! We could not let the book continue to hunt people down, even those who the whole village might agree deserve it.

It occurred to me that Opias might be able to do some scouting for me, even find the book, so I would not have to rely on Thomas's meeting with Tammy.

I pictured the book in my head. I pictured Elizabeth's farm, its fields and barn. *Opias*, I mouthed. *Look for the book. Check the barn and check the woods.*

I glanced at Tammy and jumped. She was staring at me. "What is on your mind, Violet Indian?"

"Death is on my mind," I said truthfully, hoping she did not see into my head and discover I was plotting against her.

She nodded. "Harden your heart, Violet Indian. We have only just started."

With a bored look, she turned her attention to the reverend. Though I caught her frequently looking in Thomas's direction throughout the service, he made no other motion to look our way.

Please, Opias, find the book.

I waited, hoping Opias would let me see through his eyes, but suddenly, there was a disturbance below. We all peered down, and then Ann Putnam Jr. cried out just down the bench from us. "Mother!"

We all rose, and I saw that Ann Putnam Sr. had collapsed to the floor, her chest heaving deeply and her breath rattled with phlegm.

Ann Jr. rushed down from the gallery to her mother's side as Mr. Putnam cradled his wife in his lap. "Ann!" he cried.

Everyone in the gallery crowded toward the rails as my heart raced. Mr. Putnam had voiced his fear for his family to the reverend this very morning.

Was this just a coincidence?

My vision clouded over and the meetinghouse faded from my view. There, in Mr. Osborne's barn, was Opias. He pecked and scratched away at a mound of straw, and I saw he had uncovered the book.

"Violet?" Elizabeth whispered.

I felt her grab my arm and help me sit, but I could not respond to her. "Are you all right? You're staring—staring at nothing!"

With his talons, Opias pulled away more straw and then pecked at the cover.

Open it! Open it!

"Violet?"

He scratched at the cover and then flipped the book open. He peered down and I saw the name *Ann Putnam* written on the page, where the sheriff's had been.

A rattle pierced the air, Opias turned, and I saw Bone-Shaker strike. With a loud caw the vision was broken.

"Tammy, where are you going?" Elizabeth asked.

I looked up and blinked. Tammy was racing down the stairs.

My stomach lurched. She knew I had found the book, and I knew there was no way I could follow her. How would I be able to explain my departure to Reverend Parris?

"Elizabeth, Ann Putnam's name is in the book," I whispered.

Elizabeth looked around to see if anyone might overhear

us, and we slowly separated ourselves from the other girls. "What? How do you know?"

"I saw the book, in your barn. The Putnam children will soon be motherless, and I fear Opias is dead." I clutched her hands. "Elizabeth, it's all happening so fast. I prayed we might have at least until the next full moon. And I'm sure Tammy knows I have seen the book, or she would not have left."

Elizabeth stood. "What should we do? Should I go after her?"

"Yes, but wait," I whispered. "We are going about this all wrong. We have to convince Tammy that we have indeed hardened hearts, otherwise we may never see that book. Go after her, and whatever you do, make sure she does not feel the need to hide the book again. And when you get the chance, you must rip the pages out and throw them in the fire!"

CHAPTER TWENTY-FOUR

It wasn't until evening that we got word that Mistress Putnam had finally succumbed to what those in town were attributing to wasting disease. She had been ill for much of the last year, so there were no eyebrows raised as when the sheriff had died and Opias was seen at his window.

The reverend looked troubled, though, and I imagined he was thinking back to his conversation with Mr. Putnam this morning.

I imagined he was praying hard.

I was praying hard, too. I was praying Elizabeth could get her hands on that book.

There had been no sign of Opias. When I called to him

and there were no visions or sight of him, I feared the worst—that Bone-Shaker had indeed killed him.

I was heartsick that I had led him into danger, but I figured Tammy would be quite pleased that her own familiar had killed the spy I had sent.

I wished I could go to Elizabeth and find out whether she was in possession of the book—to find out if she was able to convince Tammy we had both embraced our roles of wicked women, doling out revenge to those who deserved it.

I feared Tammy's ability to see into my head and feared she would see through the charade.

And most of all, I hoped the book would not be so quick to write another name in our blood, but given what had happened—that Ann Putnam's name had appeared, likely just after the sheriff had died—I braced myself for another death if Elizabeth could not destroy the book.

Suddenly, I heard a caw. I looked to the darkened window, wishing I were free to run outside without causing suspicion. Was it possible that was my Opias and he was somehow alive?

My heart raced as the reverend looked up from his Bible and Mistress Parris from her stitching.

"'Tis an odd hour to hear such a call," Mistress said. Her face darkened, and it was obvious she was thinking of the stories of the great black crow that had visited Lydia Corwin. "It worries me, Father."

"Shall I go out and chase it off?" I asked.

"No," Mistress Parris said. She settled back down and turned to her stitching. "You best stay inside, Violet."

I was shocked to hear a bit of concern in her voice.

"I'm sure it has flown off by now," the reverend added.

I tried to hide my disappointment and excused myself to my room. I shut my door and blew out my candle. As my eyes finally adjusted to the dark, I saw Opias's outline against the open field. Relief flooded through me.

He was alive!

I knew not how long I stared at him, but soon I realized the house was quiet. I carefully opened my door to find the house asleep. I slipped on my boots and made my way to the door.

I stepped into the night and raced to the wall where Opias was perched. He flapped to my shoulder and rubbed his head against my cheek.

"You are a lucky bird!" I said.

His talon scratched at my shoulder, and I saw a note tied to his leg. I quickly untied it, and he flew off, over the fields into the dark wood.

What is this? Who could have gotten so close to my bird?

I carefully shut the door behind me, and brought it to my room. I lit the candle and opened the paper.

My hands shook as I made out the words.

Violet,

I tried to rip the pages out, but they stayed fast. I even threw the book into the fire, but it did not burn. There is another named: your Betty. I am so sorry I failed you.

E

I paced back and forth as my heart pounded in my chest. Betty was named!

What could I do to stop the book from claiming another life? From claiming Betty's? Why had I been so stupid and reckless as to sign my name in that book—to spill my blood on its pages?

"Think, Violet!" I whispered to myself. "Think!"

How long did she have? What could I do?

Martha Wilds.

My eyes widened. She had told Tammy how to use the

book. Maybe she knew how to stop it? But Gloucester was too far to travel, and even if I could sneak off, it would likely be too late to save Betty.

Opias.

I went downstairs, walked over to the shelf, and took the reverend's journal. I carefully ripped a page out, not caring if I would be caught and whipped.

My hand shook as I wrote on the paper, and then sneaked outside again. Opias was waiting on the wall, as if he'd known I needed him, and I gently tied the note to his leg. "Find Martha Wilds in Gloucester. Do not rest until she has this letter."

Opias cocked his head and pecked at the string. "Find Martha Wilds! Go!"

Opias flapped his wings and took off. I stared back at the house, praying he could find her and that she had the answer.

Praying that I could save Betty.

I knew Opias could fly swiftly, but how long would it take for him to get to Gloucester? How could he find Martha Wilds if I did not even know what she looked like?

And what would become of Betty?

CHAPTER TWENTY-FIVE

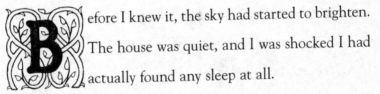efore I knew it, the sky had started to brighten. The house was quiet, and I was shocked I had actually found any sleep at all.

What if Betty had died in her sleep?

I sat up to go to her, but the room fell away.

Standing in front of me was an old woman with gray hair sticking out from beneath her dirty cap.

"What devilment is this?" she asked aloud, eyeing Opias. "Did someone send you?"

I nodded, and Opias bowed his head up and down.

Show her the note!

He cawed and bent down, picking at the twine with his beak. She cocked her head. "Is this for me?"

He cawed again, and she slowly reached out to him. "No pecking now."

She untied the note, and I watched her unfold the paper. Her eyes scanned the paper. "I'm sorry," she said, "but I am an uneducated woman—these scratch marks mean nothing to me."

My heart sank.

"Can you speak?" she asked Opias.

"*Tammy Younger*," I whispered, and Opias repeated her name in a guttural, garbled caw.

My heart soared as Martha drew back, her eyes wide. "Oh, my, my, my. This is unexpected. Are you Tammy Younger's familiar?"

"*No*," I said, and a guttural *no* came from Opias's throat.

"*The book cannot be destroyed*," he cawed.

Martha brought her hands to her chest. "Are you . . . the brown-skinned girl who was here?"

"*Yes!*" I said as tears sprang to my eyes. "*People are dying. A girl's life is at stake.*"

"Oh, my, my, my." Martha nodded, her watery red eyes filled with concern. She nibbled her lower lip. "You are right; once a book is signed in blood, it cannot be destroyed by burning or even by throwing it into the ocean.

"You need to write a new story in your book, but all must agree to it. All must sign their names, and all must spill their blood again."

Opias bowed his head.

How could I get Tammy to agree to writing a new story? She would never give up our coven willingly.

Martha grimaced. "I feared Tammy might use the book for ill purposes. I hesitated to even tell her how to cast the spell, but she said she wished merely to become a folk woman like myself. She said she wished to help you. I assumed she would use the magic to help you get to Maine to be with your parents."

My heart stopped.

My parents are in Maine?

Martha looked Opias in the eye. "Tammy didn't tell you, did she?"

I shook my head no, and Opias did the same.

I felt as if I'd been punched in the stomach. All this time Tammy knew where my parents were. She pretended to be my friend, but she only used me to get her powers . . . to romance Thomas . . . to watch families be torn apart without a care.

"Be careful," Martha whispered. "Tammy bears deep scars on her soul, and I don't imagine she would willingly rewrite her story now that she has a taste of power. What did she choose as her familiar?"

Opias cawed, *"Rattlesnake."*

Martha Wilds drew back with a grimace. "Rattler? This is worse than I could have imagined, but I can't say it takes me by complete surprise. I've never met a girl so bursting with anger. And so full of potential. Such a shame. Such a shame. Be careful." She shook her head. "No, be crafty. Tammy is a cunning one, and you will have to be craftier than she if you are to destroy your book."

She spit in her hands and rubbed them together before raising them, palms up to the sky. She breathed deeply. "I will pray the universe hears you. Folk women are healers, not killers, so I hope the power of good outshines that of the bad."

I nodded. *"Thank you."*

Opias bowed to Martha Wilds and then took to the air.

For a few short seconds I felt the cool air on his feathers, and then I was seeing through my own eyes once again.

"Mistress Parris!" Abigail shrieked. "Betty is burning with fever."

I flew from my room and up the stairs. Abigail was shaking at the foot of the bed she shared with Betty, her eyes the size of saucers, while Thomas stood frozen at her side.

I raced to Betty, but Mistress Parris pushed me away. "Stay back until we know what is wrong!" She leaned over Betty and put a hand to her forehead. "She's burning up. Violet, get some water from the well!"

I stared at Betty, who moaned softly.

"Go!" Mistress yelled to me. "Abigail, go downstairs. I will tend to Betty." She looked up at the reverend. "We heard the bird last night—the crow. What does this mean for our girl?"

Abigail cried. "You heard a *crow* in the night?" She flapped her hands in front of her chest. "Is Betty going to die like Sheriff Corwin? Am I? And look—she is breaking out in spots! It must be the pox." She looked frantic. "Will I catch it, too?"

The reverend bowed his head. "Of course not, and it is but

a coincidence we heard that bird, I am sure of it," he said, though when he looked back up, his eyes were haunted. "Go downstairs and take up a Bible and pray for your cousin."

Abigail backed away, nodding. "I will pray for her. I will pray for all of us."

I reached out and clasped her hand. "Betty will be fine; it is just a fever," I said.

Though I knew this was a lie, I also knew I would do anything I could to save her.

Abigail squeezed my hand, and tears sprung in my eyes. It had been a long time since I held Abigail's hand; it felt familiar and foreign all at the same time. We made our way, hand and hand, down the stairs.

"Thomas," the reverend said. "Go fetch the doctor. Tell him we think Betty has come down with the pox."

I grabbed the bucket by the door and waited for Thomas to come down and get his boots on, and then followed him out the door.

"Thomas, wait!" I called as he raced down the path.

"There is no time, Violet."

"I know you must go in haste, but you must listen to me

first! Betty's life depends on your hearing me out—and believing me."

He looked at me impatiently.

"It is my fault Betty is sick. I stole your father's book. Elizabeth Prince and Tammy Younger and I went into the woods under the full moon, and we formed a coven."

He shook his head. "What nonsense!"

"We wrote our names in the book and we spilled our blood and we asked the book to show us the names of those who wronged us."

"You've gone mad!"

"If only that were true! You must believe me. Sheriff Corwin's name appeared in the book, and he died that very night and then Mistress Putnam's name appeared next, and now . . . Betty's."

He shook his head.

"We have magicked familiars!" I declared.

"Familiars?"

"The crow that visited the Corwin house—that was mine. And Elizabeth has a hen and Tammy has a rattlesnake."

He scoffed. "You are either mad or coming down with fever yourself."

"It was Tammy's idea, but I went along with it. I pray God will forgive me and spare Betty. I only wished to use the magic to find my parents, but I would change places with Betty, even if it meant I would die without seeing them again. I never meant for any of this to happen, but I can show you the book and you will see Betty's name, and then you will have to believe me."

"Why are you telling me this?"

"I need you to distract Tammy. I have an idea how I might save Betty, but it will take a new story."

"New story?" He stared at me incredulously.

"Please, you have to believe me. I need you to meet Tammy out in the woods."

His brow furrowed. "I will make no promises."

I reached out to him, tears pouring down my face. "For Betty's sake, please believe me, or even if you do not, humor me. I swear to God, I am telling you the truth."

"Right now I have to fetch the doctor."

I nodded. "Later, promise me you will meet up with

Tammy, after the doctor comes."

"I can promise nothing."

"Thomas, you must meet with Tammy, or Betty will die. I just hope it already isn't too late."

CHAPTER TWENTY-SIX

homas stared at me, and I hoped he could see on my face that my wild story was true. He shook his head, turned, and ran off toward town without another word.

I hurried to the water pump and pushed the handle up and down, filling the bucket. I rushed back to the house as my mind scrambled. What were the words I needed to save Betty? What words, what story could we write in the book?

Would they even work?

I brought the water inside and took a washcloth from the pantry. I passed Abigail on my way upstairs and her lower lip quivered as tears gathered in her own eyes. When I entered the bedroom, I was shocked to see more spots breaking out now on Betty's face.

"Let me help," I said, dipping the cloth in the water.

"No," Mistress Parris said. "I don't want you to catch this. Go downstairs and wait for the doctor."

She held out her hand for the cloth and I nodded. I slowly made my way down the stairs and sat at the table across from Abigail.

"Violet," Abigail said softly. "I think God is punishing us."

I wished I could tell her the truth, but I just shook my head. "Things just happen sometimes."

Abigail bowed her head, and all at once, her body was racked with tears. "I am sorry, Violet. I am sorry about Mama Tituba, and I am sorry it has taken me so long to apologize. I do not even know why Betty and I said the things we did. We were doing the egg casting, just the two of us, and I saw a coffin in the whites! And when other girls started making accusations and people started confessing and said they could see the things we'd made up . . . it seemed the Devil really had come to Salem. We started to believe it, but . . . even your mama joined in."

She looked back up at me. "But your mama never cast a spell on us. No one ever did, but you have to believe me. I am truly sorry she is gone and that your father is gone. So many are gone. I now know God is punishing us for lying. I'm scared the black bird may come for me next, and I will have no one to blame but myself when it does."

"Abigail," I said softly.

She hung her head. "I am scared and I miss your mother and I regret every day that she was taken away. I know Betty does, too. We talk at night and wish upon the stars that we could take it all back."

"I also have done things I would take back if I could— more than you know."

Abigail pursed her lips. "When you came back from Gloucester, we could hardly look at you, knowing it was our fault she was sent away. We felt worse when your father was sent away as well." She sniffed. "I know what it is like to lose your parents. And I hate how cruelly we have treated you, Violet."

Her face crumpled. "We did not know how to say we were sorry," she cried. "And it was just easier to keep being mean. Being mean is easy. Being sorry and admitting we did a terrible thing and asking for forgiveness—I never knew it could be so hard. I don't expect you to forgive me and I know I do not deserve to be forgiven, but I am truly sorry, and Betty is, too."

Could I forgive them for what they did to my family, and the blows they dealt me every day with words that stung worse than a hornets' nest?

Could I forgive myself for the wounds I had left on two other families?

Has Abigail spent the last years wishing she could turn back the days and do them all over like I have these last few? Do either of us deserve forgiveness? I wasn't sure.

"We can try and start over," I said.

Abigail reached out and placed her hand over mine. "We will be sisters again."

I could not look her in the eye and instead focused on the hearth. "Or friends. Friends who do things they wish they could take back, but who can maybe learn to trust each other again over time."

Her cold hand squeezed mine. "I will do everything I can

to earn your trust—Betty, too. If she gets well."

"I will do everything in my power to make sure she does!"

I looked up the stairs. How much time did she have?

There was a knock and I rushed to open the door, thinking it was the doctor, but it was Elizabeth. I turned to Abigail, a finger up to my lips, begging for her silence as I slipped out and closed the door behind me.

Once outside, I turned to Elizabeth.

"I'm afraid to ask, but how is Betty?"

"She has the pox."

Her face fell. "Violet, I swear I tried everything I could to destroy the book, but the magic was too strong—fire did not even singe its cover or pages!"

I hooked an arm around hers and led her away from the house. "Where is Tammy?"

"I know not. After I confronted her in the barn, I told her I was finally ready to accept revenge on those who jailed my mother and that I was certain you would come around. She was not happy you had sent your bird to look for the book. I think she doubted my sincerity, but then I wondered aloud if Mercy Lewis's name might appear in the book and how that would be a good thing, as she was sweet for Thomas. I told her Mercy had warned me that Tammy might end up in the stocks if she kept rouging her lips. And that Mercy had used spell casting to attempt to win Thomas's affections when we were young girls. Tammy's face reddened all over, and she told me she hoped you would embrace our power, too. Then she left."

"She left you with the book?"

"Yes, that is how I saw Betty's name. I stoked the hearth and tossed in the book, but like I said, it had no effect."

"Where is the book now?"

"In the barn, where Tammy had hidden it."

"We need to get it. I have a plan to break our coven."

"Violet! Elizabeth!" I turned to see Thomas running down the road ahead of Dr. William Griggs.

"Have you seen Tammy?" he whispered, out of breath.

We shook our heads as the doctor brushed past us.

"Is what Violet said true?" he asked Elizabeth. "Have you made a coven? Is there *really* a book of names?"

Elizabeth's mouth dropped open. "How could you dare tell him?"

"Elizabeth!" Thomas yelled. "Can Tammy really command a snake?"

She nodded and bit hard on her lip. "Please don't tell your father or we shall be sent to prison or worse!"

"I have no desire to turn you in, but I was just in town. Mercy was bitten by a rattlesnake."

"Oh!" Elizabeth wailed. "I did not think for even a second that Tammy was capable of doing something like that. More blood on our hands, Violet!"

"She sent her snake after Mercy because she thought you might be sweet on her."

Thomas frowned. "They cut the wound out, but she is gravely ill. It is too soon to say if she will recover." He paused and rubbed his palm across his forehead. "Is my sister's name really in this book of yours?"

I nodded. "I am sorry to say that it is."

He looked to the house. "What is your plan, Violet?"

I reached out to him. "We must get the book and break the covenant. We will write our names again and shed our blood and I pray we can stop the madness."

"Tammy will never agree to sign her name to break our

coven!" Elizabeth stated. "Never."

I looked to Thomas and Elizabeth. "She doesn't have to agree. Tammy Younger *cannot read*. She will not know what she is signing."

"But what will we say we are writing in the book?"

"A love spell." I looked at Thomas. "Can you lure her to the woods?"

He nodded. "I hope I can maintain the pretense, though how could I possibly kiss her now, knowing she set that creature after Mercy? But I will do anything to save Betty."

"You misunderstand, Thomas. You will not be romancing Tammy. You will be casting her aside. You are tasked with breaking her heart."

Thomas drew back. "What should I say to her?"

"You will tell that when you heard Mercy was bitten, you realized how close you were to losing her—that you had always thought you would court Mercy when you got older. You must tell her you have renewed your commitment to living in a Godly fashion and you will no longer be sneaking off into the woods with her. Tell her you have asked God to forgive you for being with her. If you do this, I am certain we can get Tammy to sign the book again."

He furrowed his brow. "What if my words encourage her to send the beast after Mercy again? Or even me?"

"After you break her heart, she may very well think to do that, so *you* must be ready, Elizabeth. You must plant the seed that the only way to win Thomas back is with a spell. When she is convinced, send your hen back here to the house so I will know she is committed to the plan. We will return to the clearing tonight and hope the waning moon will still let us work our magic."

Elizabeth swallowed. "I will do my best."

"Thomas, make haste. We do not know how long Betty has before it's too late."

CHAPTER TWENTY-SEVEN

 slipped back into the house. "Any word, Abigail?"

She shook her head. "None yet. Dr. Griggs has not come down, but I have been praying."

"I as well. Let me fix us something to eat."

She rose. "I'm not sure I can manage but a few small bites, but I'll help you get things ready."

Side by side, we set the table and cut into a loaf of bread. Between bites our eyes were drawn to the stairs.

Finally, the doctor came down, followed by Reverend Parris. "She may well pull through, more do than don't. If she does, she will likely bear scars for the rest of her life."

The reverend nodded. "That is a small price to pay for her recovery."

"I will check in on her tomorrow. Keep her hydrated and cool, and I will keep her in my prayers."

He left, and Abigail brought her hand to her heart. "More people make it than not? That is blessed news; perhaps our prayers will be answered after all."

"Perhaps," I said, though I knew it would take more than prayers to save Betty's life.

"Where is Thomas?" Reverend Parris asked.

"I am not sure," I answered. "He told me Mercy Lewis had been bitten by a rattlesnake, so perhaps he is getting word on her condition."

Abigail gasped as the reverend picked up his Bible.

"He would be better off at home, praying for his sister." He turned his back to us and headed upstairs, muttering, "Ravens and snakes—these are troubling omens."

"Troubling omens, indeed," Abigail whispered after her uncle was no longer in sight. She swallowed a bite of bread and her worried eyes met mine.

"It will be all right," I assured her.

"I'm not sure I believe that is true. These are signs that the Devil may actually be here in Salem—here to punish us for lying."

I could not sit still another second. I had to find out if Thomas had succeeded.

"I will go look for Thomas and tell him he is needed at home."

"Should I go with you?"

"No, stay. I shan't be long. Mistress Parris might need you to fetch things for Betty."

"Hurry back, Violet. I do not think I can bear it alone down here for long."

I rushed to the door and then turned. "Abigail?"

"Yes?"

"I forgive you and Betty."

She bowed her head. "I know not that I deserve it, but thank you."

I nodded and headed out the door. I raced down the road and found Thomas looking ashen at the edge of the wood.

"It is done?" I asked.

"It is done."

I noticed a welt across his cheek. "Did she strike you?"

He touched the spot and shook his head. "No, she simply reached out to touch me and it was like she had fire in her fingertips. I think you should go to them; I am not sure

Elizabeth will be able to contain her."

"I will go at once!"

"Wait! What's the word on Betty?"

"Dr. Griggs said there's a good chance she would recover."

Thomas looked grim. "The doctor knows not of your book."

I peered up at the afternoon sun. "Evening cannot come fast enough."

"Good luck, Violet."

"I will need it!"

The long road to Elizabeth's flew by in a blur as I ran, ignoring the stitch forming in my side. As I approached the farm, I could hear heated words coming from the barn. I slowed my approach and caught wind of Tammy in a rage.

"I will send Bone-Shaker to her room tonight when all are asleep and none can intervene to save her this time."

"What is going on?" I asked, feigning ignorance.

"You have to reason with her," Elizabeth pleaded, picking up her hen.

"What has happened?"

Tammy threw her arms in the air. "Mercy Lewis has

happened! I sent Bone-Shaker to teach her a lesson for mocking me and what happens? Thomas Parris has decided he is in love with her!"

My eyes darted to Elizabeth's. "Well, they have always been very fond of each other. We had always assumed they would wed—until *you* came along."

Tammy balled her fists. "Well, that is the plan once again!" She stamped her foot and dust rained down from the rafters. "She will take her last breath tonight!"

"Whoa!" I said. "Tammy, wait. If something happens to Mercy, do you really think Thomas will come back to you? Or will he mourn her and *harden* his heart? He could even be so despondent that he leaves Salem to stay in his new mentor's house, and you might never see him again."

Tammy started to pace, sparks flying from her fingertips.

"I told her we could cast a spell!" Elizabeth said meekly. "A love spell."

"I do not want to win his love through a spell," she spat. "He needs to want me above all others without magic. I know he can again—if Mercy Lewis dies."

Elizabeth and I exchanged glances.

I reached out to Tammy. "What if we cast not a love spell, but something opposite? Instead of making him fall *in* love with you, we make him fall *out* of love with Mercy."

Tammy scoffed. "I do not want to win him through magic! He has kissed me and held me and I already know I have his heart. I just need Mercy out of the way, and then he will meet me in the woods again. He will smile at me at services so everyone knows he is mine."

"Tammy," I said. "Thomas Parris cannot smile at you at services. It is not proper and you are years away from courting. But we—"

She turned to me. "But what?"

"But we can harden Mercy's heart toward Thomas, right? We can make her fall out of love with him and then he will be—"

"Free to come back to me!" Tammy began to pace. "He would think only of my kisses and surely forget about Mercy. Violet, you're a true folk woman!"

I exhaled. "I am feeling more and more like a true witch—I am feeling more and more that the world will be ours to mold, one spell at a time."

Tammy smiled. "I am sorry I doubted you, Violet. And I am sorry I sent Bone-Shaker after your bird. I thought you aimed to destroy the book. It is a good thing your bird has quick reflexes."

"Praise be," Elizabeth whispered.

"I merely wished to see if another was to be named," I explained. "I am pleased Betty Parris will finally get her comeuppance for destroying my family."

"She breathes still?" Tammy asked.

"For now," I answered.

Tammy snatched the book from on top a pile of hay bales and opened it. Relief flooded through me to see Betty's name still written in blood—for if her name were still there, she was still alive.

Tammy touched each red letter, one by one. "For now, indeed. And now we must make plans to meet in the clearing again. Bring Opias and that ridiculous hen of yours, Elizabeth. We will cast a spell to make Thomas Parris forget all about Mercy Lewis!"

"How should we do it?" Elizabeth asked.

I touched Betty's name and then shut the book. "We will

use the second page. Elizabeth, you will write down the spell and we will all sign our names like before."

"And then we'll cover Mercy Lewis's name in our blood," Tammy said gleefully.

CHAPTER TWENTY-EIGHT

lizabeth paled. "Yes, she will be sorry she spoke out against a member of our coven."

"I should go back to the reverend's house," I suggested.

Tammy folded her arms across her chest. "Send Thomas my regards!"

"You can send them in person soon enough," I noted.

"I will indeed! Wait, where *is* your bird?"

My heart raced as I thought of speaking to Martha Wilds through Opias this morning. I quickly pictured him looking through the Corwins' window, hoping that if Tammy Younger could indeed reach into my mind, she would see that image instead. "I sent him to the woods. The town is aflutter that he is an ill omen, and I do not wish to see him harmed by someone eager to snuff out his life with buckshot."

Tammy narrowed her eyes and cocked her head. "Bring him to the barn."

"But why?"

"Because I feel you are perhaps hiding something."

My stomach lurched. "I know not what you mean," I said, careful to keep my voice steady.

Elizabeth stared at me from behind Tammy. I had not had time to tell the whole story of Martha Wilds to her, but it was clear she knew something was amiss.

"She really should get back, Tammy. If she is missed, it might make it harder for her to sneak out, and we have no cows giving birth tonight."

Tammy looked back and forth between us. "I think the Parris household will be preoccupied with Betty tonight and will pay no mind to Violet. Are you sure Opias is in the wood?"

I stood tall. "Yes."

She folded her arms across her chest. "Bring him here. Now."

"Opias, come!" I called out.

I said a silent prayer that he was back from Gloucester. I walked out of the barn into the yard and searched the sky. "Opias," I whispered. "Please, please be near."

To my relief, I heard a caw in the distance and saw him soar in over the treetops and land on the barn roof.

"I'm not sure what that was all about," I sniffed, "but if you are so interested in my bird, perhaps you could have chosen one as your own familiar instead of that worm of yours!"

"I am quite happy with my choice, thank you very much," attested Tammy. "We will see you tonight and I'm dying to hear how your Betty is faring. She seems to be lasting longer than the others, which is too bad, as I am eager to see the next name."

I don't know why I was shocked at her callous words, but tonight couldn't come fast enough. I turned without saying goodbye and headed down the road. "Meet me at the clearing, Opias. I will be there after dark."

As I made my way back to the house, I wondered what would happen to Opias once the coven was broken. Would he simply vanish? Or perhaps he would become closed off to my mind. I would miss him, but it was more important that we stopped the chain of death, because I now knew it was likely only a matter of time before Mama's name would appear in the book.

Maine.

I had hardly any time to ponder that Mama and Papa were in Maine, but now that I knew, I wondered if I could buy my freedom from the Parrises? Would they let me go?

I wish I had more time. I could have magicked more coins to help pay for my freedom, but I knew in the end, it was more important to end things with Tammy.

At least when the time was right, I now had a direction to go in: north.

I approached the house and found Thomas sitting on the rock wall. "How did it go?" he asked quietly.

"Well, my original plan fell through. But then I convinced her we were not casting a love spell on you, but instead we were casting a *falling*-out-of-love spell on Mercy Lewis. Tammy is convinced you will then find your way back into her arms."

He blushed.

"I am sorry, Thomas. I shouldn't have been so blunt."

"And I should never have fallen for the likes of Tammy Younger."

"We can both agree to that. How is Betty?"

"More pox have appeared. She is still feverish, but hanging on. Mother looks like she's aged twenty years just since this morning. Violet, I have never seen anything this frightening."

"I am sorry I brought this plague to your house."

"Violet, I know what Tammy is like, but I know you wouldn't have written in that book if you knew what would happen."

"I would like to think that is true. Thomas, do you know where in Maine my parents are?"

He cocked his head. "How do you know they are in Maine? Father refused to tell any of us where they were going. In truth, it is likely even he does not know. I can see him not caring enough to find out when the man purchased your parents."

"Someone told me they were in Maine. One of these

days I will leave Salem and find them."

"I will do anything I can to help—even if it means sneaking you out under cover of night."

"No, when I go it will be in the light of day and I will have earned my passage north in a way in which God and my parents would be proud of."

He nodded.

"I need to check on Betty. I need to see her suffering so I can chase the fear from my heart, firm my resolve, and take on Tammy Younger tonight."

"Will you and Elizabeth be safe?"

"If we are not, we only have ourselves to blame, and it's a risk we have to take."

"I can come with you."

"If Tammy were to see you, she would know we were laying a trap. I thank you for your concern, but this is something Elizabeth and I need to do alone."

"I understand, and I will be praying for you tonight."

"Save all your prayers for Betty, for she is the one who needs them most."

I walked into the parlor and Abigail still sat at the table, her bread unfinished. "She is getting worse." Tears streaked down her face. "She looks so *awful* and her breath is so labored."

I looked out the window, willing the sun to set so we could put our spell in motion. I walked up the stairs with fresh water and peered into Betty's room. The reverend was kneeling by the side of the bed, clutching his Bible while Mistress Parris softly wept. I took a few steps closer and stifled a gasp.

Betty was unrecognizable. Every inch of her was covered with pus-filled sores, and I struggled to make out even a glimpse of her delicate features underneath it all.

Mistress Parris looked at me. "Violet, you shouldn't be in here."

I nodded. "I am so sorry."

She bowed her head. "All we can do is pray for her, Violet, but I fear we may lose her."

I wondered, if Tammy could see Betty, would she still wish to continue our revenge scheme? I hoped she would not, but Tammy Younger had indeed hardened her heart, and I felt even seeing Betty like this would make no impression.

I could not fail tonight. "I am so sorry," I whispered

again. "I am praying for Betty. What can I do to help?"

Mistress nodded. "Violet, there is nothing you can do. Please go. I could not stand it if another in this house were to fall ill."

For the first time I saw compassion in her eyes, perhaps being so close to losing Betty had opened her heart—even if just a little.

I turned and raced downstairs and burst into tears. Abigail came to me and took me in her arms. "We have lost so much time, with our foolishness and lies, Violet. I am so sorry."

"It seems there are enough apologies here to sink a ship," I said between sobs.

"I don't think Betty is going to make it," Abigail confided.

I wanted to tell her she was wrong, and Betty would pull through—but I was not so sure anymore.

CHAPTER TWENTY-NINE

I paced in my room, waiting for the sky to darken. If only it had been winter, I could have made my way to the woods an hour ago. Thomas and Abigail sat at the table, their stew cold in front of them.

"It's getting late, Violet," Thomas called out, tilting his chin to the window.

It suddenly occurred to me that I was to share my bed with Abigail. She would notice if I left. Would she try to stop me?

I decided I had to be honest with her—well, as honest as I could be. I walked to the table and sat opposite her. "Abigail, I will be going out soon, and I may not be back for a while."

"Going out, with Betty clinging to life? Where are you going?"

"I cannot tell you where, but if your parents ask, you must say I am asleep."

"How can you go out into the night when there are ravens and snakes out and about haunting the town?" she implored.

"I'm going to try and help Betty."

Her eyes widened. "How can leaving the house help Betty? Oh!" Then she whispered, "Can you work magic like Mama Tituba did? Magic to save Betty?"

"I don't think my mama had real magic—but I do. I want to get rid of it, though—but not before I can help Betty."

Abigail shook her head. "How can working with the Devil help Betty?"

"I have never met the Devil, nor do I plan to. I am more of a folk woman."

"Like your mama?"

"I have seen some things that would make Mama's hair stand on end. But, yes."

Abigail shuddered. "I don't think you should do it. It's

asking for trouble and I'm pretty certain we have enough of that right now."

"Let her go, Abigail," Thomas said softly. "Violet knows what she is doing."

Abigail turned to her cousin. "You know of this plan, Thomas? Does it have anything to do with the burn on your cheek?"

Abigail reached out, and Thomas winced when she touched the raw, red streaks. "It does."

She stared at us and then rose, taking off her cap. She pulled a metal hair comb from her long locks and handed it to me. "Wear this so I will be with you while you save Betty."

"You are not afraid that I will be practicing witchcraft?" I asked.

She took my hand. "If Betty is cured, I think even the reverend would not find fault with you."

"I am not so sure about that."

Abigail sniffed. "Well, even if the reverend were to find fault, I *know* God would not."

She squeezed both my hands now. "Go and hurry and work your magic! Just come home as soon as you can so I can keep my heart from leaping from my chest."

"I will."

"And I will fix the bed so it looks like you are already asleep."

"Thank you, Abigail," I said as I slipped on my cloak and slowly opened the door.

The moon was still more than three-quarters full and bright enough to illuminate the path through the fields. Even if it had been pitch-black, I was sure my feet would have found the way. I rushed on, faster and faster, Betty's pox-marked face ever urging me on.

I wound my way around trees and over decaying logs, and finally in the distance came to the clearing with the lit fire. I heard Bone-Shaker rattle his tail, and instead of filling me with fear, it filled me with anger.

This would end tonight.

I quieted my steps using the folk-woman way and noiselessly made my way closer to the fire. I searched the branches until I spotted Opias. *Fly*, I mouthed. *Make noise!*

I crept up behind where Tammy sat and called out, "I'm here."

Opias swooped down from the trees, cawing loudly.

Elizabeth screamed, and Tammy jumped to her feet.

"What you do that for?" Tammy demanded.

"I didn't scare you, did I?" I asked.

"No," Tammy said flatly, though I knew that had indeed unnerved her.

"Yes!" Elizabeth squealed. "My heart is about to give out!"

I wanted to keep Tammy unnerved so she wouldn't read my mind. Our plan had to go off without a hitch.

"Let us not waste another moment," I declared. "I am eager to use our powers again."

Tammy's face warmed to me. "As am I." She turned to Elizabeth.

"Me as well," added Elizabeth. "You deserve to have Thomas Parris all to yourself."

Tammy sat, and Elizabeth and I joined her on the forest floor.

Tammy handed Elizabeth the book, and she opened it to the first page. I exhaled. Betty was still named, so at least that meant she was still alive.

"You seem not so disappointed to see your *friend* still draws breath."

"She is suffering," I said, hoping my lie would satisfy Tammy.

Elizabeth held a pencil in her hand and started to write.

"Stop," Tammy said. "I will tell you what to write."

Elizabeth licked her lips. "Of course, it is your spell."

"*We three on this new night do command the book to do our bidding.*"

"So many words," Elizabeth complained.

I watched Elizabeth carefully and saw that so far, she was writing down what Tammy said, word for word.

My body shook.

Tammy spun around with her arms out. "*And we command that Mercy Lewis fall out of love with Thomas Parris.*"

I held my breath as Elizabeth's hand began to shake and I saw what she was actually writing.

We command that our coven shall be irreparably broken, the book destroyed, and that Tammy Younger shall be stripped of all her powers. Forever.

"Anything else?" Elizabeth asked, her voice close to breaking.

"Read it back to me," Tammy said.

Elizabeth's eyes widened, and I knew she was trying to

remember all that Tammy had said. "We command that Thomas Parris fall in love with—I mean out of love with Mercy Lewis."

Tammy peered into Elizabeth's face. "Why do you quake so?"

"I remember how frightened I was when we first used the book. Do we have to bury it again, or just spill blood? I am anxious to get this done and over with."

"We must write our names first and then drip the page with blood."

Elizabeth nodded and hurriedly scribbled her name across the page. She handed me the pencil, and as I formed the letters, I realized our mistake.

Tammy's name was already on the page, and even if she didn't know her letters, she would see that it was *her* name and not Mercy Lewis's that Elizabeth had written.

My own hand was still shaking, and Elizabeth's eyes widened as she took Tammy's hand and wrapped it around the pencil.

She looked at me and I could not be sure whose heart was thumping louder.

She hastily dragged Tammy's hand across the page and

then slammed the book shut, before Tammy could see her own name scrawled. "Now, for the blood. Give me the knife, I will go first," Elizabeth chirped.

Tammy took the small knife out of her pocket but drew it back. "Since when are you so eager to draw blood?"

"Since I have embraced my wickedness!" she said unconvincingly.

Tammy stood and looked at Elizabeth and me. "What is going on?" Tammy demanded.

"We are casting a spell on Mercy Lewis," replied Elizabeth, without meeting Tammy's gaze.

Tammy snatched the book from Elizabeth and opened to the page. Her eyes rapidly moved down the page and then she growled, "What did you write, Elizabeth Prince?"

"I wrote just what you asked."

"Liar! And *you!*" she said, turning on me. "You knew what she was doing! Did you really think I would not see my name written twice on the page?"

I held out my hands. "It is not what you think, Tammy. It is true we did not write the spell to turn Mercy from Thomas. We wrote the spell so Thomas would fall in love with you, as originally planned."

Tammy's shoulders softened. "Why? That is not how I want to be with him."

Elizabeth shook. "We—we thought this was the only way to guarantee Thomas would be yours. There are other girls in town—proper girls."

Tammy clenched her jaw. "There was a time when Thomas Parris loved that I was not a proper girl."

I nodded. "Truly, we thought this was the only way to be sure that Thomas would be yours."

"Yes!" Elizabeth nodded her head rapidly. "We were only thinking of you. We just want you to be happy."

Elizabeth laid the book on the ground and touched a finger on Tammy's name. "We shouldn't have kept it from you."

Tammy folded her arms across her chest. "No, you shouldn't have, but perhaps you are right. I know Thomas did love me and I am sure he was just shaken after Mercy was bitten. Perhaps I drove him into her arms. Perhaps I was too impulsive."

"Yes, you can be impulsive." Elizabeth smiled weakly. "Let's finish the spell."

Tammy handed Elizabeth the knife.

Elizabeth grimaced.

"You did say you wanted to go first."

Elizabeth took the knife and winced as she made a cut across her thumb. She then painstakingly squeezed three drops onto her name.

An icy wind sailed past us, bringing chills to my arms.

Tammy's eyes darted around.

"The spell is working already," I said hurriedly. I took the knife and sliced my thumb. As each drop of blood hit my name, the wind grew.

"This doesn't seem right," Tammy said.

"Just do it!" Elizabeth commanded. "Unless you are suddenly frightened of a little blood . . . or a little wind."

Tammy snatched the knife from me and threw it into the darkness. "Something isn't right. I will not put my blood on this page."

Elizabeth stared at me. "Violet, please do something—or all is lost."

Tammy pushed Elizabeth, knocking her to the ground. "Lost? What are you trying to do? What does the spell really say? Tell me or I will kill you!"

Bone-Shaker lunged at Elizabeth, and she screamed as her hen flew in between them. The snake clenched the bird in its jaw, shook it, and then tossed its limp body aside.

In shock, Elizabeth froze. "You can't mean it, Tammy! You just killed my hen. Would you really kill me?"

Tammy shook her head. "Tell me or you will not be as lucky as Mercy Lewis. I will send my snake after you, and hold you to the ground until the venom takes your life— just as it did your hen's."

"Tammy," I implored. "We knew not how the spell would come to us. It is a love spell, that is all."

Just then Elizabeth screamed out, "Violet, the book!"

Tammy and I looked down and saw that the book was smoking by some unseen fire. Tammy's mouth dropped open. "Martha Wilds had said the book would be indestructible. She said . . ."

Tammy stared at me.

"You had your bird spy on Martha Wilds. I knew it. You are a fraud. You wanted to destroy the book all along. But how—how is this happening?"

"Tammy, it's not what it seems!" I said.

"Don't lie to me, Violet Indian, I can see it on your face. You always did give yourself away with your soft, pathetic heart. I will kill you both and I will shed no tears. I will find new girls—hard girls, who would never betray me."

Suddenly, Thomas Parris stepped out of the shadows with a shovel and brought the blade down on Bone-Shaker's neck, severing the snake in two. The pieces wiggled and danced as Elizabeth screamed in horror.

Tammy went wild and threw herself at Thomas. "What have you done?" she shrieked, pounding on his chest.

He threw her to the ground. "I am saving my sister." He leapt down and pinned her shoulders back while she writhed and screamed, trying to throw him off.

"Elizabeth, get the book!" I called out. I took the metal hair comb from behind my ear and dragged it deeply across Tammy's arm. Blood welled up as heat and static leapt from her body.

"I can't hold her much longer," Thomas yelled.

With a strength I didn't know I had, I yanked Tammy's arm and held it fast over the book. "Come on! Just three drops."

The first landed on her name, and the book pages flapped in the icy wind, blowing smoke in my face. I squinted, trying to make sure I could get two more drops on her name. "Elizabeth, hold the pages down!"

Drop number two landed on its mark, and flames leapt from the page, melting some of my hair.

"Hurry, Violet!" Elizabeth cried.

The final drop hit the page and the book's spine snapped in two. The pages rose in the air and burned, leaving ashes all around us.

"What have you done?" Tammy screamed. "What is happening to me?"

Her hair stood on end as lightning left her body, crackling into the night air.

"What have we *done*?" Elizabeth glared at Tammy. "We have broken the pact and stripped you of all your powers."

Tammy knelt on the ground, sobbing. "But . . . why?"

I shook my head. "Despite all the terrible things that have happened in my life, I could never enjoy seeing someone else suffer. Never. We could not abide it a day more."

Elizabeth put her hands on her hips. "I suggest you make

your way back to Gloucester. I will inform my stepfather that you simply took off in the night."

She turned to Thomas. "Do *you* want me to go?"

Thomas inhaled. He nodded, giving her an unflinching stare.

"But I love you."

"I don't think you are capable of loving anything. If I ever see you in Salem again, I will confess to all we have done in the woods. We will be put in the stocks, but it will be worth it."

"I don't believe you, Thomas," cried Tammy. "You can't mean it."

Thomas coldly turned his back. "I need to go home to see if my sister still breathes—not that you care."

Tammy stood and brushed herself off. "I don't care. Your sister and Abigail and all the others deserve what they get. And, Violet, good luck finding your parents without the book."

"Martha Wilds told me that they are in Maine. She told me you knew."

She sneered. "I did, but I am most happy knowing that

without our magic, you will never have enough coins to pay off the reverend. Your parents may as well be on the moon, as you will never see them again. I for one will sleep very well every night knowing this. You could have had anything you wanted."

Tammy rubbed the cut on her arm and spat on the ground. "Goodbye, Violet *Indian*."

She turned and walked rapidly away. Soon she was engulfed in the dark woods.

"Let's go home," Thomas said softly. "We'll walk you to your farm, Elizabeth."

"No, we must go see Betty," she said. "I must see if destroying the book worked."

"Even with the book destroyed," said Thomas, "she may not be out of danger yet."

I bowed my head. "Let's hope and pray that she is." I looked at the snake's body, which was still twitching, and Elizabeth's poor hen. "I plan never to set foot in this clearing again."

CHAPTER THIRTY

t services that next Sunday, Reverend Parris spoke of the power of prayer and how it had taken Betty from the brink of death to cured in one day's time. Never satisfied, he also took the opportunity to chastise the congregation for letting his kindling box go empty and complain about the lack of tithings keeping him from buying even a new book to compose his sermons in.

But when Thomas, Elizabeth, and I had arrived back at the house the night we broke the covenant and sent Tammy on her way, Mistress Parris and Abigail were weeping with joy. The pox that had covered Betty were gone by half already, and in the morning, she was clear of all lesions. Dr. Griggs said it was indeed proof that leading a Godly life could bring miracles.

I thought it was proof that sometimes you have to make your own miracles.

Some in town still talked of the black bird that went to Lydia Corwin's, and that she was forced to bury her husband in the basement of the house for fear his grave would be desecrated. But overall, it felt as if a dark cloud had been lifted from the town, and people seemed more at ease.

Thomas and I were questioned as to what we were doing out that night and we had said, *praying,* in unison.

With Betty's miraculous cure, none questioned us further.

This Sabbath, though, I was nearly jumping out of my skin for the sermon to be over. It had been almost a month since Tammy Younger had left Salem to who knows where. Without the magic of three girls—three women—Opias was spending more and more of his time in the woods, and there were days he did not answer my call at all, but this morning I found him waiting patiently on the rock wall with a note tied to his leg:

Violet,

You must come to my home after services. I have news that will change both our lives. This is the magic we have been waiting for.

E

With permission from Mistress Parris, as soon as the reverend concluded his last *Amen*, I ran all the way to Elizabeth's. She was sitting on the front step, holding a leather bag. When she saw me, she leapt up and met me halfway.

"Violet, the governor of Massachusetts has sent money to the families of those who had been wrongly accused of witchcraft and died."

"Money?"

She shook the bag. "My stepfather has been talking of selling the farm. I persuaded him to give me half of the governor's money on the condition I move on and leave him with one less mouth to feed and no claim to anything from the sale."

My heart sunk. "You're moving? This was not the news I was expecting. I am happy for you, but . . ." I tried to hold back the tears threatening to spill from my eyes.

She shook her head, all the while beaming at me. "We are moving."

"What?"

"Violet, I am giving you the money to buy your freedom, but on one condition. You must let me accompany you to Maine. There we can be independent women and pioneers . . . and we can find your parents."

My hand flew to my heart. "I can't ask you to do that."

"You saved my life, Violet. You gave me hope and you deserve to get out of that house and I couldn't be more happy to share this with you. Both of our mothers were victims."

"But my mother—"

"Your mother did not know what would happen when she told those stories any more than we knew what would happen when we signed our name in that book. Do you really think your mother would have said all she did if she knew what would happen?"

"I don't think so—I hope not."

"Well, let's go to Maine and ask her."

"Elizabeth, are you really sure you want to go north? You've heard the tales of attacks from savages and wolves, and really, I couldn't ask you to sacrifice your coins and maybe even your life for me."

She stood with her chin raised and an air of determination on her face. "I will not take no for an answer. I am *ready* to leave this town and start fresh, and I require a fearless partner who can think on her feet and protect me from wolves—and snakes."

I grabbed her hand, a rush of giddiness sending butterflies fluttering in my stomach. "Are we really to go to Maine?"

Elizabeth laughed. "We really are. We need to go speak with the reverend, though, but given the talk in the town about his finances, he may be very willing to let you go. I can feel it, Violet, very soon you will belong to no one but yourself."

I buried my face in her shoulder and my chest racked with sobs. "I will see Mama and Papa again. Will they even recognize me?"

Elizabeth hugged me tight. "Of course they will."

I drew back. "How will we find them, though?"

"People would have heard of an Indian couple—seen them."

"Opias! Maybe we can send him ahead. He doesn't always obey me anymore, but it is worth a try." I looked at the purse in Elizabeth's hand. "Is this a dream?"

"A dream come true."

***

Three weeks later Elizabeth and I stood in town in the early morning ready to board a wagon to Maine.

"I can't believe you're really going," Betty said, weeping. "I feel like I just got you back."

After Betty was fully recovered, we three girls took to sleeping in Mama and Papa's bed. I felt a great sadness about parting from them, as it was a very cold house I was leaving.

Abigail dabbed her eyes with a handkerchief. "I will miss you, but hug Mama Tituba the moment you see her and tell her it is from me—and tell her that I am sorry."

Betty nodded, and we fell into a group hug.

Mistress Parris sniffed. "That's enough, girls, you're

making a spectacle of yourselves." She looked down at me. "You will be missed."

I half smiled at her attempt at warmth. "You as well."

Thomas reached out and patted my shoulder. "Write if you are able."

I nodded. "I know not what to expect, or if they even have paper where I'm going. If I am able, I certainly will, but all of you will be in my hearts forever."

The wagon driver cleared his throat. "I have a schedule to follow here, folks. Let's get a move on. I need to clear Gloucester by dark."

Elizabeth and I turned to each other, our eyes wide. She reached for my arm in alarm.

"Clear Gloucester?" I asked. "We won't be stopping there?"

"No, there is a barn we can sleep in about four miles past town. I have some supplies for the landowner, and he lets me water and feed the horse and sleep under cover. It won't always be so hospitable, though. I hope you girls know what you're in for."

"They are tougher than you think," Thomas said.

"I'm still not comfortable bringing unaccompanied girls up to Maine, but I can't turn down the money."

I looked at Reverend Parris, who stood a few feet away from the wagon, and he gave me a brief nod in farewell. I suppose I should be grateful that he was allowing me to leave. When Elizabeth showed him the money to pay for my freedom, he was hesitant. Mistress Parris had grown frail over the past year, and he was a man used to owning slaves since his days on his plantation.

Betty and Abigail had promised they were more than capable and could easily handle the chores, but perhaps there was a beating heart with some feelings in the reverend's chest after all.

Or perhaps he was simply moved by the money.

There were rumors that people were gathering evidence to get the reverend removed from his post. Tithings had dried up by half, but heading to Maine, I knew I might never find out what would become of him and the family.

I knew Reverend Parris held no sway over me now, though. I wanted to forgive him for what he had put me through, but perhaps my heart was not quite that big. My only regret in leaving was that Betty, Abigail, and Thomas would remain in that cold house while I could finally be my own person.

The man helped Elizabeth into the cart. He looked at me and then back at Elizabeth. "She your girl?"

"She is nobody's *girl*, and she has the papers to prove it."

I unfolded my paper and handed it to the man.

"Violet North? That's your name? Funny, we just happen to be going north."

"The stars gave me my name."

The man's brow furrowed, and he looked to Elizabeth as if I might be mad. "Well, Violet *North*, you may come in handy if we run into some Indians along the way. You can talk to 'em."

"My skin may be brown, but my people are not from around here—not even close."

He looked me up and down and then spit brown tobacco at the ground, just missing his feet. "If you say so, *Miss North*—I am sorry to hear that, though."

"I'm sure my parents were sorry to have to leave their home so many years ago."

The driver blinked twice and then drew back, as if he were trying to process what I'd just said. "I was just hoping you could come in handy," he said finally. "Word from Maine is that things are getting bad."

He held out his hand and helped me into the cart.

"Pay him no mind," Elizabeth whispered. "Some people think the world is just here in Massachusetts."

I nodded. "It is so much bigger than that. Maybe after we find my parents, we can go south. Or to Europe! Why should we stop exploring?"

Elizabeth placed her hand over her heart. "One step at a time, Violet North. One step at a time. I am putting on a brave face, but a part of me is scared. Salem is all I have known. Not that much of it has been pleasant, but what guarantee do we have that life will get easier where we are going?"

"There are no guarantees, but our conviction to be our own masters—a servant and an orphan farm girl—heading out into the unknown for a better life, that is all that matters. We didn't need a book of spells to get out from under the thumbs of all those who oppressed us—we just need to be brave. I cannot promise we will live happily ever after, but we will live on our own terms."

Elizabeth and I nestled between boxes and blankets and our few meager belongings. As the cart pulled away, we waved one last time to the town of Salem. It was time for our adventure to begin.

***

Days later, night fell, and Elizabeth and I cast our gaze to the stars lighting up the sky.

"Which one is your star again?" Elizabeth asked.

I pointed to the brightest in the heavens. "That one, the North Star. Papa said sailors use it to help navigate their ships."

"It's beautiful."

"And it's shining down on Mama and Papa right at this very moment."

"And Tammy Younger," Elizabeth said.

I nodded. "If Tammy is looking up at the stars right now, I hope she can feel their light and I hope they can bring her some peace."

"Do you think that it's possible for Tammy to find peace?"

I sighed. "Probably not." I thought of the reverend. "It seems like peace just avoids some people whether they be holy men or witches."

Elizabeth squeezed my hand. "Hopefully, we will find peace up in Maine—or at least the opportunity to make something of ourselves."

"We will weave a new kind of magic, the kind only strong, independent women who are brave enough to travel on their own to Maine can. I thought that book was going to be the answer to our prayers, but the answer was inside us all along—we just had to go to hell and back to figure that out. At least now we can tell our own story."

EPILOGUE

hree days into our journey, I woke from the bumpy ride, hearing Opias cry out in my head. The road and the wagon had vanished, and I was perched in a tree, looking down at a small log cabin.

Opias was picking at the note I had tied to his leg.

"John! John, come quick! There's a raven out here—it's in the tree and it's holding something. No, something is tied to its leg."

My heart swelled.

Mama!

He had found her. I was afraid he'd just fly off on his own, but he found her.

Opias flew to Mama's feet and bowed. Mama bent down and untied the string. She opened the paper and fell to her knees. "John, it's from Violet! I watched her write her name so many times there is no forgetting it, but I can't make out the rest of it. *John! Get out here!*"

Papa rushed to her side. "From Violet?" He took the note and read it with wide eyes. "She's coming to find us—she's free."

"Free? How can that be?"

Opias cawed.

"It doesn't say," Papa whispered.

Mama reached out and clutched his arm. "Praise be this bird. It must be a forest spirit from home—our *real* home." Mama frowned. "This bird found us, but how can Violet find us?"

Papa looked up at the last stars shining in the brightening sky. "Our Violet will find *us*. The stars will show her the way."

ACKNOWLEDGMENTS

This book could not have been finished (and no lie, it was a nail-biter) without the help of my sister, Kerry Malloy, and my daughter, Meredith, for reading and commenting and being the kind of people who are really good at grammar and constructive criticism and listening to me cry when things got hard.

My husband, Joe, went above and beyond and had my back and was so very supportive during this process—he did most of the weekend shopping and laundry and cooking. He's always done a lot of this stuff anyway, but we try to split it up—you know, divide and conquer—but during the writing of this book he did so much more so I could squirrel myself away in my office. And while he is quite capable at laundry—it is not his thing (it's not really my thing either)—but he did it, week after week. So thankful for this guy! Love you!

Thanks to Max Marrone for being an all-around great son and helping out whenever you could.

And then there are my pirates, ahem, cohorts: Robin McCready, Susan Colebank, Angie Frazier, and Patty—aka Trixie—Murray with her endless supply of pies and moments when I actually think she is serious, and I might have to wrestle her in the mudflats of the Damariscotta River in Maine.

Robin, you are our pirate queen, but you all fill my soul and encourage me to keep going—our weekends have untangled so very many writing knots over the years that I cannot begin to thank you enough.

Nina Nelson—you have been here from the start and you've always had my back. Sometimes I need your advice and cheerleading more than anyone's.

I want to give a shout-out to Karen Eaton, Lesa Visser, and Gretchen Webster and so many of the other English teachers at Shelton High School—I was blown away by the seven months I was able to watch these professionals teach and inspire and enlighten their students every day. Their use of books and media to make novels accessible to students of all abilities was inspiring. My children have fond memories of so many of their English teachers at Shelton High, and I was so happy to have the opportunity to see so many of them in action while I was working there.

Ladies who have been in and out of room 15 this year and last—Amanda, Sam, Kaitlyn, Melissa, and Mary—thank you for being supportive as we take things one day at a time.

Thank you to Anne Heausler for a really great copyedit! You were on the ball and so helpful!

And huge, magical thanks to my agent, Rick Richter. If you look up *optimism* and *have-your-back*, you will find Rick's name and picture. And thank you so much for steering this project toward me and for all your help when I was floundering.

And then there is my editor, Sonali Fry. This was her baby. She wondered about the Salem witch trials, the people left behind, and most of all she wondered about how Violet Indian's story might have evolved with a little help from magic. With so little known about what happened to Tituba after the witch trials and less known about Violet, she entrusted me to research the history and tell a story that could have been. I read so many books, took so many notes, and then imagined.

Thank you, Sonali, for planting the seed, and most of all, your patience.

AUTHOR'S NOTE

When I was in fifth grade, I had to choose a nonfiction book to write report on. I ended up picking a book on the Salem witch trials. I don't remember much else other than I got a good grade and I developed an interest in this dark part of our American history.

My interest in the occult in general was no surprise. I grew up in an old, creepy house with a father who loved to tell ghost stories, and the Salem witch trials were just so fascinating to me—young girls claimed they were bewitched by their friends and family, and people confessed to doing the bewitching.

This was not something that happened every day.

Abigail Williams was a real person and it is said she actually reached into the hearth in her home and picked up hot coals in her hands while being "bewitched." Tituba's confessions are on record as she told of flying on poles to Boston and being told to sign the Devil's book.

In my young mind, these accounts seemed a good case for believing Abigail Williams could possibly have been truly afflicted.

But as I read more and more books about this subject matter as I grew older, it seemed obvious to me that Abigail Williams was lying, or there was something other than witchcraft that was causing her behavior. Some have even theorized that a fungus in the rye flour used for making bread could have caused the delusions some of the girls suffered, but as I delved deeper into the topic, it seemed human nature's baser instincts came into play during that time. People used the witch trials as means to settle petty grudges, steal land and other property from those accused, and punish neighbors who were different.

When I was asked to write the story of Violet, the daughter of Tituba, I knew I had to go further into what I had previously read about this time period. Tituba was an enslaved Indian who lived in the Reverend Parris's house and one of the first accused of being a witch. While there is no clear evidence about where Tituba was born and what happened to her after the governor of Massachusetts pardoned all the accused, my readings led me to concur with several historians that Tituba was an Arawak Indian originally from South America.

Tituba, Sarah Good, and Sarah Osborne were all accused of afflicting Betty Parris and Abigail Williams on February 29, 1692. Both Good and Osborne denied any wrongdoing. Osborne died in prison and Good on Gallows Hill with a noose around her neck.

Tituba's confession of practicing witchcraft seemed to be the catalyst that led to other civilians joining in with the mayhem—be they accusers or those who confessed to witchcraft to keep from being taken to Gallows Hill. Her accounts of meeting with the Devil and his human minions are on record and seemed to feed the witchcraft fever.

I pored over books about Tituba, the trials, Salem, and Dogtown, which was once a part of Gloucester,

Massachusetts. The characters named in the book are based on real people—Reverend Parris, Sheriff Corwin, Martha Wilds, Ann Putnam—but I played with some of their time lines to fit the story I created for Violet as I imagined what it would be like to be the daughter of the first woman to be accused of, and then confess to, practicing witchcraft.

Tammy Younger's time line is perhaps the one I tinkered with the most. Being born decades apart, she and Violet would never have crossed paths in real life. But Tammy Younger was known as the "Queen of Witches" in Dogtown—a now-abandoned village of Gloucester—where it was rumored she cast spells on travelers and behaved in unseemly ways for the time.

Bringing Tammy together with Violet and her real-life contemporaries, Betty Parris, Abigail Williams, and Elizabeth Prince, allowed me to explore these questions: What if there really was a kind of magic people could tap into that had nothing to do with the Devil? What if that magic could help expose the lies and deceit? What if that magic could test some of those vulnerable girls and lead them to make choices about how they could live their lives under the shadows of death and betrayal—and possibly break free from them?

My hope is that readers will ponder the answers to these questions and more after reading this piece of historical fiction.

FOR FURTHER READING

Breslaw, Elaine G. *Tituba, Reluctant Witch of Salem: Devilish Indians and Puritan Fantasies.* 4th ed. New York: New York University Press, 1996.

Foulds, Diane E. *Death in Salem: The Private Lives Behind the 1692 Witch Hunt.* Guilford, Conn.: Globe Pequot Press, 2010.

Goff, John. *Salem's Witch House: A Touchstone to Antiquity.* Charleston, S.C.: The History Press, 2009.

Hill, Frances. *Hunting for Witches: A Visitor's Guide to the Salem Witch Trials.* Beverly, Mass.: Commonwealth Editions, 2002.

Schiff, Stacy. *The Witches: Suspicion, Betrayal, and Hysteria in 1692 Salem.* New York: Back Bay Books, 2015.

Starkey, Marion L. *The Devil in Massachusetts: A Modern Enquiry into the Salem Witch Trials.* 24th ed. New York: Anchor Books, 1989.